EAGLES OVER CANAAN

EAGLES
OVER CANAAN

EDWIN DARYL MICHAEL

quarrier
press

Charleston, WV

Charleston, WV

ISBN 13: 978-1-942294-69-6

Other Historical Fiction By Edwin Daryl Michael

Shadow of the Alleghenies
Death Visits Canaan
The Last Appalachian Wolf
Coyotes of Canaan

Cover photograph: © Linda Freshwaters Arndt, freshwaters-arndt.com
Back cover photograph: © Judd H. Michael, Penn State University

Distributed by:

West Virginia Book Co.
1125 Central Ave.
Charleston, WV 25302
www.wvbookco.com

TABLE OF CONTENTS

ACKNOWLEDGEMENTS

I am indebted to Julie Dzaack for her conscientious efforts to assure the biological and geographical accuracy of this novel, as well as her encouragement and thoughtful comments in making it more readable.

I am also grateful to Rich Bailey (WVDNR), for providing historical nesting data for West Virginia bald eagles and to Matt Overton (Dominion Energy) for providing historical nesting data for Mt. Storm Reservoir bald eagles.

And I am especially appreciative of the advice, critique, and thorough editing provided by Sean Edward Michael. His in-depth analysis converted my rough draft into a refined novel.

viii

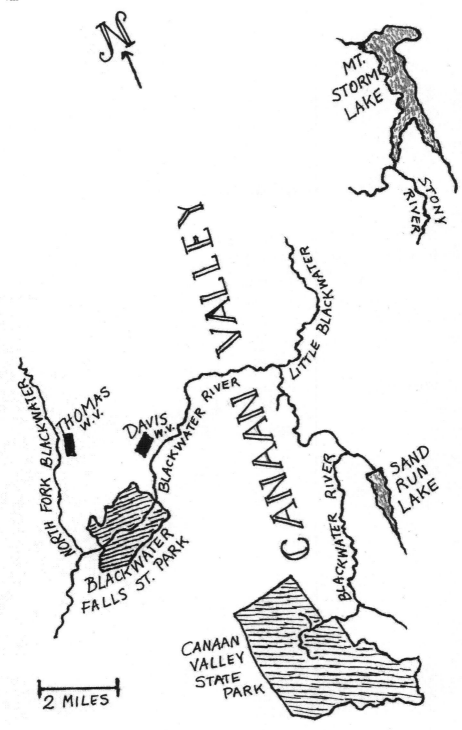

Courtesy of Nancy Jane Callander

INTRODUCTION

I observed my first Tucker County, WV bald eagle in 1988, while conducting a raptor survey in Canaan Valley as part of a long-term study to determine the impacts of the proposed Davis Pump Storage Power Project on wildlife. From 1981 to 1993, my team of five biologists monthly drove all roads in the Valley and recorded all crows, ravens, vultures, and raptors (hawks, falcons, and eagles) sighted. The only bald eagle our team spotted during that 13-year period was the one in 1988.

Helicopter surveys conducted three times a year during the same 13-year period covered all major waterways, beaver ponds and man-made ponds, and lakes in Canaan Valley and adjacent Dolly Sods, plus the entire perimeter of nearby Mt. Storm Reservoir, had only two bald eagles sighted: one in November 1990 and one in November 1991. Equally unproductive were thousands of ground-based surveys conducted by my team from 1978 to 1993. In addition, I never spotted a bald eagle while spending thousands of hours behind a Brittany Spaniel in pursuit of ruffed grouse and woodcock in the Valley for three decades, starting in 1975.

I became a part-time resident of Canaan Valley in 2002 and completed a detailed telemetry study of snapping turtles throughout the Sand Run and Glade Run watersheds. These facts, coupled with a lack of any historical records of sightings, convinced me that no resident bald eagles existed in Canaan Valley during the 1900s—only nomadic birds wandering through the area.

Not until 2015, did I begin seeing adult bald eagles in the Valley. One snowy day, I excitedly watched a pair of adults sitting together in a red spruce, then discovered the first bald eagle nest in autumn 2016. Most hardwood trees had dropped their leaves and the broad bulky nest caught my eye from over 250 yards away. I had been wandering along tributaries of the Blackwater River in search of brook trout, and the nest was in the forks of a black cherry tree on the hillside about 35 yards from the stream.

Although no adult bald eagles were detected that autumn day, I returned the following March while snow still blanketed the ground, and was rewarded with the sight of an adult standing on the rim of the nest. Both elated and cautious, I remained some 400 yards away, and studied the bird through a spotting scope for nearly an hour. Although I could not see into the nest, distinctive incubating behavior by the adult convinced me that eggs were present.

I observed the nest in alternating weeks until May, at which time I reluctantly concluded the pair of eagles had abandoned their nest. It was at that time I began to focus my observations on the Blackwater River, man-made lakes, and beaver ponds, with the goal of documenting the first successful bald eagle nest in Canaan Valley. My definition of success was simple: a nest must produce eggs, nestlings, and, ultimately, fledgling eaglets.

Golden eagles were even rarer in Canaan Valley than were bald eagles. From 1975 to 2000, I am aware of only one golden eagle that was spotted. I was riding in a helicopter conducting surveys. The mature golden eagle was the first I had ever observed from above. Only when observed from above and behind does a person fully comprehend the basis for the bird's common name. It was a beautiful sunny November day, and the head and neck feathers of the bird almost glowed in the bright light. The helicopter pilot maintained a wide separation to avoid alarming the bird but our survey schedule forced us to soon leave the majestic bird.

This book is fictional, but it is based on documented facts and personal observations compiled over 40+ years. All events described in the novel were witnessed by the author or were reported by biologists. Although identities of humans featured in the novel have been changed, names of geographic features follow accepted local terminology. The fundamentals of the events surrounding the first successful Canaan Valley bald eagle nest, as reported in this novel, are as true-to-life as I could possibly make them.

I spent over 400 hours directly observing bald eagles in Canaan Valley between 2017-2022. The majority of observations were made with a variable power spotting scope (15X-60X) from a cabin where I reside part-time. All field observations, including those involving active eagle nests, were aided with 12X binoculars and a 20X spotting scope. Following guidelines of the U.S. Fish and Wildlife Service, I approached no closer than 200 yards to an active nest.

To better understand bald eagle behavior during egg laying, incubation, and rearing of eaglets, I studied the live video feed of a pair of bald eagles with a nest along the Monongahela River, south of Pittsburgh. My focus was primarily on the close-up videos covering the 2021 and 2022 nesting seasons, made available on line by the Audubon Society of Western Pennsylvania in cooperation with PixCams.com.

CANAAN'S FIRST EAGLE NEST

The sky was blue!
The snow was bright!
The bird was big!
It was an eagle—a bald eagle!

The mature male eagle was soaring over a lake in the southern end of Canaan Valley, closely studying the fish cruising in the shallow waters below. The size, wingspan, and black and white plumage of this bird created a most striking scene. Visible from distances of up to half a mile, a flying eagle quickly grabs your attention. The bright yellow feet, ebony black talons, wicked beak, and glaring eyes function as magnets to grab a human's attention.

That day was one of those crystalline, spring-like days that occur rarely as winter gradually comes to an end. Snow was melting on small patches of south-facing hillsides, and shorelines of ice-covered beaver ponds were showing open water. Ramps were pushing their shiny green tips up through the winter-flattened leaf litter. Choruses of croaking wood frogs drifted out of the ephemeral ponds so essential to their existence. Canada geese had recently returned from North Carolina and pairs were defending their chosen nest sites. And red maple buds were emitting a pinkish glow, promising that spring would soon arrive.

Amidst this backdrop, the male eagle's mate was sitting atop three eggs, the first-ever laid in Canaan Valley. She had been incubating the eggs for 14 days, and had another 21 days to go before they hatched. The nest was fully 60 feet off the ground in a black cherry tree. The black cherry tree would leaf out in April and provide a canopy for the eaglets. Bald eagles almost always select a live tree for their nest as tree foliage is essential to their survival. They would be hidden from view of harassing crows and red-tailed hawks. Gusty winds, freezing rains, and hot rays of the spring sun would be moderated. The eagle pair had begun constructing their nest as snow fell in early November. Then on February 13, the female laid her first egg. The second and third eggs were deposited at two-day intervals.

The two eagles had become a dedicated, committed pair the previous autumn, when the mating urge arose, and by October the male had selected their nest tree. He began carrying sticks and small branches to the tree, and interwove them to form the foundation. Throughout October he continued construction with the female occasionally joining in. Nearly 100 sticks were utilized in nest construction during September, followed by 75 more in October, 25 in November, 20 in December, another 20 in January, and over 50 in early February.

Most winter days, the eagle pair spent half the daylight hours searching for fish, and the other half constructing their nest. Both eagles became proficient at spotting fallen branches and carrying them to the nest. They also learned to identify suitable dead limbs in the forest canopy, and to break them off by landing firmly atop each one.

By February, the nest was nearly five feet wide and over three feet deep, and weighed 500 pounds. With the base structure completed, the male devoted entire days to searching for fish and patrolling the pair's territory of nearly two square miles.

Meanwhile, finishing touches were being put on the nest. The male carried fistfuls of small twigs, dried leaves, tufts of grass, and clumps of moss to line the nest. To make it even more comfortable, the female pulled half a dozen feathers from her breast. The sticks and twigs forming the inner walls of the nest were shaped into a broad bowl, while the floor contained a cup-like depression, approximately 12 inches in diameter and four inches deep.

The construction phase was completed in January, and during February the female spent short periods each afternoon, sitting quietly in the nest. During this time, she squirmed constantly, steadily conforming the depression to her shape. Her presence also declared to every crow, raven, and vulture passing overhead that the nest was occupied.

With the completion of the foundation in December, serious interactions between the eagle pair occurred daily. Nest building instigated courtship and the strengthening of bonds, which in turn led to copulation.

Courtship displays during January often occurred while the pair were perched in trees, but more commonly while they were flying. With one bird perched on a favorite tree branch, often overlooking Sand Run, the mate would soar in and land a few feet away. One bird would sidle close to the other, often making physical contact. Vocalizations frequently accompanied courtship, with one or both birds throwing its head back and screeching loudly.

Despite this bold behavior, perching courtship was typically quite subtle, and only noted by other eagles – and curious wildlife biologists. In contrast, aerial displays were one of the most spectacular events to occur in the lives of the eagles. Typically, the two birds pursued each other in wild, unique, high-in-the-sky performances. Rapid, steep dives were common, each bird flying to a great height, folding its wings, and plunging towards earth at speeds reaching 100 mph. The pair only pulled out of the dive a few yards above earth, and headed back to the clouds, where another dive was initiated.

Courtship chases often involved cartwheel displays, in which the pair flew 1,000 feet skyward, locked their talons together, and tumbled towards earth – twisting and turning in one cartwheel after the other. Of course, they always disengaged before crashing to earth.

Copulation occurred solely on tree limbs, never while flying. The female solicited the male. She crouched low, assumed a horizontal position with wings slightly apart, and called to her mate. At times, she nudged the male to inform him of her strong desires.

In response, the male emitted his own mating call, flapped his wings, and jumped lightly onto the back of the female. When the female twisted her tail sideways, the male pressed his cloaca to hers – the "cloacal kiss." Sperm were ejected by the male each time the two cloacae met, and the largest and most viable sperm moved quickly up the oviduct towards the waiting eggs. Copulation typically lasted only ten seconds, but at times, the act persisted up to two minutes.

Copulation occurred twice on February 7, seven times on February 8, and two times the morning of February 11. The first egg was deposited in the nest depression at 5 p.m., February 13, as darkness settled over the valley. The second egg appeared on February 15 and the third on February 17. Now began the 35-day incubation period. The first bald eagle eggs in Canaan Valley rested comfortably in the eagle-sized cup, totally covered by the soft, insulating feathers covering the female's breast.

While the female incubated, her mate fished and stood guard. Although he brought fish to his mate most days, on occasion the female departed the nest. At those times, the male assumed incubation duties. Relief from the long periods of inactivity in the nest was necessary for the female to stretch her flight muscles, but it also provided her the opportunity to soar high over the Valley – an activity she greatly enjoyed. And, of course, she was also provided the opportunity to do a little fishing.

The male had selected a tall red maple, slightly uphill from the nest, as his primary lookout tree. Nights were spent perched on one particular horizontal limb, 40 feet above the ground and providing an excellent vantage point for viewing his mate. It was four inches in diameter, an excellent size to encircle with his powerful talons and toes. He slept soundly, often with his head tucked beneath a wing.

In contrast, the female seldom remained asleep for longer than 30 minutes at a time. She constantly turned each egg, an instinct that assured proper development of the encapsulated embryo. While standing astride the eggs, she would pull each egg back beneath her breast with her curved beak. With much wriggling, she positioned her breast feathers and thigh feathers around the eggs to assure protection against cool night air. At least 20 times each night she awoke, rolled the eggs, repositioned her own body to face a different direction, and resettled over her eggs. Similar to the male, she typically slept with her head beneath a wing.

Alarm calls from the female, or unusual sounds near the nest immediately woke the male. He typically responded with a reassuring, high-pitched cry. If he detected no signs of danger, he returned to sleep.

Both parents alternated incubation and egg-turning duties during daylight hours, turning them one or two times per hour. Throughout a 24-hour period, the eggs were typically turned three dozen times.

The hillsides surrounding Canaan Valley were dominated by hardwood trees, including black cherry, red maple, sugar maple, beech, and birch, while the Valley floor was relatively open. Extensive areas of goldenrod, grasses, and ferns were intermixed with patches of alder, St. John's-wort, and blueberries, plus a few small stands of quaking aspen.

The male was aware of every white-tailed deer near the nest, but ignored them. He also followed the flight paths of crows and ravens, and the less frequent hawks and vultures, as they cruised the Valley in search of food. Because none of those large birds were a threat, he ignored them also.

That unseasonably warm February afternoon, the female was basking in sunlight atop her three eggs, as a yearling black bear was moseying along underneath. The bear had emerged from winter hibernation the previous week, but had no success finding food yet after his three-month slumber in a small cave on Cabin Mountain. Because of the deep snows atop the mountain, he had wandered down to the Valley floor, and focused his foraging on the beaver ponds and small tributaries of Glade Run and Sand Run. Digging into a muskrat house had resulted in the capture of one muskrat, but the three-pound meal did little to reduce the bear's hunger pangs.

The bulky nest was high enough off the ground that the bear was unaware of its presence. His attention was focused on the partially-dried head of a small creek chub, discarded by a mink the previous night. After eating the fish head, the bear began searching for other foods. With his head held high, and nostrils flaring wide, the black-furred bruin sorted through the multitude of scents for one that promised a meal.

A black bear's power of scent is a hundred times more effective than that of a human. Scattered about the base of the black cherry tree were a few fish heads and bits of fish skeletons that had dropped from the nest above, plus numerous splashes of eagle excreta. Although the fish carcasses contained only tiny bits of dried flesh, the bear picked up their scent and maneuvered up the steep hillside to the base of the nest tree.

The male eagle had brought his mate a full-grown white sucker during late morning. The alluring scent of fresh fish had drifted earthward, and the black bear eventually concluded it was coming from overhead. Normally, the bear would never have been enticed to climb the tree but hunger forces animals to do unusual things. Although lean and weighing just 90 pounds, the young bear was strong and agile enough to climb the tree. The scaly bark of the black cherry provided an excellent surface for his inch-long claws. In less than ten minutes the bear was almost within reach of the nest.

Ice had covered the beaver ponds, and the male eagle was fishing the Blackwater River where the water was open about half a mile away on the day the black bear arrived at the nest. The female eagle heard the bear climbing the tree, and flattened herself even tighter over the eggs. Although unable to see the bear, she sensed his progress as inch-long claws broke the brittle cherry bark.

The moment the young bear pulled himself up into the first fork that supported the nest, the female eagle lunged at him. The startled bear recoiled, but only for a minute. As the eagle violently thrashed her wings at the head of the bear, she emitted high-pitched alarm calls. Although her three-inch long talons would have injured the bear, she did not attempt to strike him solidly. She was hesitant about getting too close to him and did not want to move too far from her eggs. At every attack, the clinging bear opened his jaws and attempted to bite the eagle. His clacking teeth further enraged her, and she intensified her attack.

After nearly four minutes, the hungry bear realized the eagle would do him no harm, and he gripped the edge of the nest with the claws of his right front foot. Just as he pulled himself onto the edge of the nest, the male arrived. Having heard his mate's desperate call, his response was immediate. Skimming over treetops at 30 mph, he initiated a rapid dive aimed directly at the bear's head. However, instead of strafing the bear, the male crashed full force into its head. One talon pierced an eye, a second pierced an ear, and the bear squalled in pain. Losing his grip on the nest, the bear tumbled backward into the tree's fork. He managed to grip the trunk, but slid downward 15 feet before arresting his fall on a sturdy side branch.

The eagle had reflexively pulled his talons from the bear's head as the marauder began his fall. As the bear came to a halt, the eagle pair resumed their attacks. Bleeding and half blinded by the two raptor's sudden strikes, the bear quickly backed down the tree to the ground. Unrelenting, the male eagle's continued attacks sent him scampering down the hillside. With his eyesight nearly ruined, he gave out a few bawls, then galloped towards the headwaters of Glade Run.

The female returned to her vigil, resuming incubation of Canaan Valley's only three eagle eggs. Air temperatures had been in the 40s during the short time the female eagle was off the nest, and so the eggs suffered no damage. The potential for the Valley's first eagle eggs to hatch into eaglets was still promising.

EGG INCUBATION

Following the encounter with the black bear, the female redoubled her dedication to incubation duties, constantly keeping her eggs dry and warm. The eggs, which had originally been white with light tan flecks, had now faded to a soft beige color. Whether faced with wind-driven cold rains, pelting sleet and snow, or bright sunshine, she huddled over her clutch. The nighttime shift was her sole responsibility, while the daytime shifts were shared. Three to four times each day the female ventured off the nest and searched for fish.

The eagles maintained egg temperatures at 105°F. Both adults had a constant body temperature of 106°F and developed a small featherless brood patch, which assured skin-to-shell contact to maintain critical egg temperatures day and night.

Although the female was frequently disturbed by flying squirrels, which are strictly nocturnal, no real threats occurred during the first three weeks of incubation. However, the serenity of the night was disrupted shortly after midnight on the eleventh day of March. Temperatures had fallen the previous day, and a skiff of snow covered the forest floor. Both eagles were asleep, motionless and seemingly headless, with a wing as usual providing comfort. The cloudless sky glittered with countless stars as the full moon cast distinct shadows across the forest floor.

The stillness of night was broken by a shriek of shock and pain from the male. He had been attacked! A solid blow to his left shoulder had loosened his grip and knocked him off the perch. He tumbled to earth, a cartwheeling flurry of wings and tail, and found himself lying atop the snowy leaves. His shoulder had been bruised, but was functional, and he sprung aloft, returning quickly to his perch, alert to identify the culprit.

Amidst the Valley's January snows, an abandoned broad-winged hawk's nest, itself covered by a cap of white, had been commandeered by a male great-horned owl and his mate. With only slight modifications, it had proven quite acceptable to the female and so the orbit of their territory was set.

Although the two nests were perched in treetops nearly 200 yards apart, the owls often flew past the eagle's nest during their nocturnal hunts. The owls were well aware of the eagles and their nest, just as the eagles had studied the owls and their confiscated nest. And if memory of a passing owl was not adequate, the deep, soft calls of the owls echoed through the woods nightly, reminding the eagles of their neighbor's presence. For their ferocity and physical strength, great-horned owls are referred to as "Tiger of the Woods" in most of North America.

The female great-horned owl had been incubating a pair of eggs for 30 days, and the first egg had hatched the previous night. The male great-horned felt an increased urge to protect the owlet, the unhatched egg, and his mate. His feeding foray that night when the first egg hatched happened to carry him towards the eagle nest, and his excellent night vision enabled him to spot the sleeping eagle from a full 80 yards distance.

Despite the great-horned owl's impressive stature – three pounds in weight, 24 inches long, with five-foot wingspan – it was significantly smaller than the bald eagle's nine pounds, 43 inches length, and six-foot wingspan. However, what it lacked in size it more than made up for in ferocity. Equally important, extremely soft feathers enabled the male to dive almost silently and his short, wide wings allowed him to maneuver efficiently between the black cherry trees. The attack was initiated from a towering red maple 60 yards uphill from the sleeping eagle. Great saucer-like eyes, the largest of any creature living in Canaan Valley, focused on the sleeping eagle.

Tightly-clenched talons, toes, and feet formed a pair of solid fists, which struck the eagle solidly. Rather than trying to kill the eagle, the owl had instead hoped to shock it into abandoning that particular stand of trees. The eagles, it felt, were much too close to his own nest. Closed talons had prevented the owl from gripping the eagle and engaging in deadly conflict – a battle the owl most likely would have lost. Struck with the force of a spiraling football, the eagle emitted a shrill screech as it tumbled off its perch.

In the darkness above, the female eagle immediately raised her head, but did not move from the eggs. Her main responsibility was to protect them, not to aid her mate. The owl passed unnoticed beneath the eagle nest, while behind him the male eagle flew back to its perch.

Within minutes, however, the owl repeated its stealthy attack, and the male eagle was again knocked to the ground. This time, however, he flew to the nest tree and landed on a limb, eight feet from his mate. Soon both resumed normal nighttime sleep behavior, drifting off after a few reassuring calls. As if on cue, minutes later the male eagle was once again knocked off the bough by the persistent owl. And, undeterred, again the eagle returned to the nest tree.

At night, owl eyesight is much better than that of all other creatures, including a bald eagle's. Despite this advantage, the owl, bruised by the third encounter, retreated to his own nest tree where he relieved his mate of incubation duties. The male eagle remained in the nest tree the remainder of the night, but never lowered his guard by tucking his head beneath a wing.

There were no more confrontations between the Sand Run eagles and owls that year. Each adjusted to the presence of its neighbors, and both resumed their partial isolation – eagles feeding during daylight and owls under the cover of darkness.

Soon the first two weeks of March passed, as did March 20, the date the eagle's eggs should have begun hatching. The female, with assistance from her mate, continued to incubate her eggs, turning them several times daily to maintain even heating, and to assure the embryos did not stick to the shell. With the passing of March 25th-28th, the female began spending several minutes every hour standing alongside the eggs, rather than sitting atop. She continued gently rolling them with her beak several times every hour, but with considerably less enthusiasm.

Normally, within 30 days of egg-laying she would have detected sounds from inside each egg, but no such "announcements" were received. Her incentive to incubate the three eggs weakened with each passing day as her instinctual clock sensed an overdue event. Her mate joined her several times daily, emitting low chirps of encouragement, as she walked incessantly around the rim of the nest. Both adults were perplexed and frustrated, sensing something was amiss.

Instinct told them there should have been some activity, some life, within the eggs. But there were no sounds emanating from the eggs, no signs of egg-shell pipping, and no signs that down-covered chicks would be emerging from the eggs. By April 3, two weeks beyond the 35-day incubation period, the female began spending long periods perched on the rim of the nest. By April 10, much of her daylight hours were spent at Sand Run Lake – away from the nest entirely. At first, the male sat on the eggs when his mate exited the nest, but eventually he, too, was no longer drawn to the nest.

By the first of May, when eagle nests in the Ohio Valley and nearby South Branch Valley contained fully-feathered eaglets, the lone Canaan Valley nest supported no life – no adults and no chicks. It grew more barren still when a pair of ravens discovered the highly-visible, pale-white eggs later that week, and carried them back to their own nests, where the undeveloped yolks were fed to hungry chicks.

Canaan Valley's first bald eagle nest, a milestone in the area's natural history, had been a failure. Yet, the silent, massive nest remained, one part memorial, another part potential future home.

MOUNTAIN STATE BALD EAGLES

The first bald eagle nest in West Virginia was discovered in Hardy County in 1981, overlooking the South Branch of the Potomac. The nest was upstream of Romney, now a terminal for the Potomac Eagle Scenic Railroad. That same pair of eagles returned to the nest in 1982, and successfully fledged two additional young. The nest was successful nearly every year during the 1980s and 1990s, producing fledglings that eventually matured and returned to the South Branch Valley as adults.

The second successful West Virginia nest was located 45 miles away as the eagle flies, in Grant County, in the Smoke Hole area of the Potomac River in 1987. It was active for 20 years, however there has been no recorded activity since then. In total, 10 eagle nests were documented in the Potomac River basin of West Virginia in 2000, and 11 in 2001.

An eagle nest was constructed on Blennerhassett Island, in the Ohio River near Parkersburg, in 2001. However, it was not successful, and the adults did not return. The first confirmed successful eagle nest outside the Potomac River was in Hancock County, along the Ohio River, in the northern panhandle in 2006.

The West Virginia Division of Natural Resources (WVDNR) monitors bald eagle nesting in the state, and documented 36 active nests in 2010, 73 in 2015, 113 in 2020, 75 in 2021, and 81 in 2022. Successful nests have been located in 31 West Virginia counties, with the majority in Grant, Hampshire, Hardy, Mineral, and Pendleton. Each of these was along or near the South Branch of the Potomac River. Nonbreeding adults, however, have been seen in most counties. By 2020, most major rivers in West Virginia had attracted bald eagles and supported active nests. These included the Bluestone, Cheat, Greenbrier, New, Ohio, Potomac, and Tug Fork rivers.

By comparison, Canaan Valley does not contain a major river, being drained instead by the smaller Blackwater river which seldom exceeds 25 feet in width and four feet in depth. At many locations, it is less than 12 feet wide and two feet deep. Beaver dams alter the flow at numerous locations, too. The resulting, elongated pools provide suitable fishing habitat for bald eagles and play a role in attracting them to the Valley.

Canaan Valley is a 35,000-acre, oval basin, consisting of a relatively flat valley floor averaging 3,200 feet in elevation, and surrounded by mountains reaching 4,000 feet. The Valley stretches 14 miles long by a mere three miles wide, and tilts slightly to the north. The headwaters of the Blackwater River flow in the southwest corner, joining several other tributaries as the main river meanders north, before eventually turning west and passing through the town of Davis. From there the river flows westward, cascading over Blackwater Falls before joining the Dry Fork to form the Black Fork of the Cheat River near Parsons.

The northern section of the Blackwater River, where the river is largest, flows through the 16,000-acre Canaan Valley National Wildlife Refuge. No human dwellings are adjacent to or near the banks of the Blackwater River throughout the northern three-fourths of its lazy, winding path through the Valley. By contrast, in the southern one-fourth of its drainage, where human structures are present, the river is too small to provide nesting or foraging for bald eagles.

In its natural state, even with the presence of dozens of beaver ponds, the majority of the Valley scarcely provides enough habitat for bald eagles. Existing bodies of water, and their fish populations, are simply too small to attract large fish predators. Not only are the populations too small, but most fish living in the Blackwater River and its tributaries are too small to satisfy the needs of a bird as large as an eagle. Beaver ponds typically cover one-half acre or less, although there are a few complexes, such as that along Glade Run, that reach four or five acres. Those ponded bodies support more large fish (12-20 inches) than do the slow-moving waters of the Blackwater and its tributaries.

Ironically, artificial bodies of water, such as farm ponds, water treatment ponds, golf course ponds, private ponds, and man-made lakes provide the most productive foraging habitat for eagles in Canaan Valley. These impoundments contain numerous bluegill sunfish, largemouth bass, white suckers, and brown bullhead catfish. Sand Run Lake, situated within Timberline, a vacation home development, provides near-optimal foraging habitat for bald eagles.

A 300-acre "conservancy" area surrounds Sand Run Lake and its headwaters, assuring that wildlife can live relatively undisturbed within a wide band of natural habitat. The lake is 30 acres in size, contains large fish populations, and has dozens of large black cherry and red spruce trees around its border.

Optimal foraging habitat for bald eagles is characterized by numerous, large, "perch/search" trees. Although eagles spend considerable time soaring over bodies of water in search of fish, they spend many more hours simply perched on a sturdy, nearly horizontal limb studying nearby waters for a potential meal. Preferred perch sites provide an unobstructed view of the water, plus a clear pathway to launch themselves over the water. This unobstructed view also enables an eagle to study the behaviors of crows, turkey vultures, and other bald eagles. Concentrations of these birds, when associated with low swoops or dives earthward, alert eagles to a potential meal. If a dead fish or a dead deer is discovered by a crow or vulture, any bald eagle within one mile will soon investigate the carcass.

Canaan Valley was denuded by loggers during the early 1900s, and subsequently scoured by fires and heavy grazing from cattle, horses, sheep, and white-tailed deer. Decades further on, these processes have resulted in a scarcity of suitable, large "eagle" trees near the Blackwater River. The tree-felling behavior of beaver lent its own demise of large trees.

Bald eagles most likely visited Canaan Valley during the late 1900s, as they migrated to and from northern nesting sites in adjacent counties. However, none was ever reported to have built a nest in the Valley. And why would they? The South Branch of the Potomac River lies only 20 miles east of Canaan Valley, a 30-minute flight for an eagle. However, the adults that nested along the South Branch during the 1980s and 1990s apparently spent little, if any, time in Canaan Valley.

I first witnessed multiple adult bald eagles in the Valley during the winter of 2015-2016. Two mature, white-headed, white-tailed adults were sighted several days that winter, circling over Sand Run Lake in search of fish. They became more numerous every winter from 2015 until the present (2023).

Historic records of bald eagles in western Virginia and West Virginia are extremely rare. I know of no written reference to bald eagles in this region until the late 1900s. Eagles, both bald and golden, were present throughout sections of the Central Appalachians in the 1700s and 1800s. However, their presence apparently prompted no mention in historical writings that mention bison and elk, mountain lions and timber wolves. Was the bird heralded as our national symbol so common that the writers of the 1700-1800 era believed their presence not worth noting?

We can assume that a few bald eagles were present in West Virginia in the 1700s and 1800s, because an examination of place names reveals at least 15 sites in West Virginia with the word "Eagle." We have, for instance, the enduring names of Bald Eagle Hollow, Eagle Bend, Eagle Branch, Eagle Rock, and Eagle Run.

Yet across North America, bald eagle habitat had begun declining during the 1800s and continued to do so through the first half of the 1900s. In addition, thousands (probably tens of thousands) of the noble birds were shot for sport and for bounty, resulting in The Bald Eagle Act being passed in 1940 to provide federal protection throughout the United States (except for Alaska). Of equal significance to eagle populations, water quality declined dramatically during the mid-1900s, resulting in significantly lower fish populations. The future of bald eagles appeared dark during the 1960s, but not solely from habitat loss or hunting.

Wide-spread use of the chemical pesticide DDT to improve agricultural crop production resulted in egg-shell thinning in bald eagles. A near total lack of successful reproduction resulted, and several prominent ornithologists predicted that bald eagles were headed for extinction. However, after the use of DDT was made illegal by the federal government in 1972, eagle populations began to slowly recover. A half century later, bald eagle populations are now greater than when DDT use first began.

The U.S. Fish and Wildlife Service announced in 2022 that bald eagle numbers had quadrupled since 2009, and was officially numbered at about 350,000 birds. This is an amazing comeback for a species that was thought to be facing extinction only 50 years earlier, and whose lifespan is 20 to 30 years.

EAGLE SUMMER

Characteristic of most bald eagles, the Canaan pair that built the first Valley nest in 2016 were mated for life. They had committed to defend one another against danger and to share all duties involving nest building, egg incubation, and protection of eggs and young. They also had an equally strong drive to feed and nurture each year's eaglets: a four-month marathon process.

Following the failure of their first clutch of eggs in 2017, the solid pair bond that had been so prominent during the reproductive phase became somewhat loosely structured. Many days they "fished" together, both sitting in the same tree. More commonly, they were in separate trees and searching different stretches of water for unsuspecting fish.

They saw one another every day in July, following the abandonment of their eggs, but one morning in August, the female ventured west to the Dry Fork River. The following week, the male moved east to the South Branch River. For nearly three months, they remained separated, each having no difficulty catching two or three fish per day.

On the fifth day of their separation, the female eagle, hereafter referred to as "Talona," discovered a juvenile osprey soaring high above the Dry Fork River. The osprey was a yearling, hatched from a nest along the Chesapeake Bay the previous year. Similar to all young osprey, the yearling had spent the previous 12 months wandering aimlessly. Initially it followed the Atlantic Coast south through Maryland, Virginia, and North Carolina. In September, it had headed west, eventually reaching the Tennessee River, which it followed to the mighty Mississippi. From there it leisurely headed downstream until reaching the Gulf of Mexico. It lingered in coastal Louisiana and Texas before flying south to Panama, where it wintered with thousands of other osprey that had spent the summer in Maryland and neighboring states.

In March, the young osprey began its return trip, eventually reaching the Chesapeake Bay the first week of April. Talona was sitting in a river birch, when she spotted the osprey soaring over a placid stretch of water several hundred yards downstream.

Bald eagles are quite skilled at capturing fish, but they lack several traits that make ospreys more successful. An osprey has proportionately longer wings and a lighter body, and can soar and hover with less effort and dive to greater depths than can an eagle.

Talona studied the osprey as it dove into a deep pool. With outstretched feet and legs, the black and white osprey went completely under water. When the bird emerged with a thrashing trout, the bald eagle immediately pushed off, heading in a beeline towards the osprey. Before the osprey had an opportunity to land, Talona was 70 feet overhead. The osprey spotted her and dived closer to the water. The eagle closed the distance to less than ten feet. The osprey's five-foot wing span nearly equaled the six-foot wingspan of a bald eagle. However, the osprey weighed only three pounds, hardly a third of the adult eagle.

Fearing the larger eagle, the osprey dropped its fish and flew downstream. Talona deftly grabbed the fish before it reached the water, and soared back to the birch tree. With one foot firmly anchoring the fish across the branch, Talona began ripping off chunks of fish flesh. As usual, she began at the head. Her hooked beak tore off jaw bones, head bones, gills, and eyeballs. Every segment was quickly swallowed, including not only bones but also fins. In less than six minutes, the eagle had consumed the entire trout, concluding by swallowing the forked tail. The hungry osprey responded by flying downstream and around a large bend, where it resumed its hunt, well out of sight of the eagle.

Talona's mate, Piercer, meanwhile had encountered a juvenile bald eagle soaring over a pool of the South Branch River, in Hampshire County. The juvenile male was four years old, and had not yet attained the mature black and white plumage of an adult. It was dark brown all over, and more closely resembled an adult golden eagle than an adult bald eagle. Piercer closely observed the juvenile for nearly two hours as it soared, unsuccessfully dove into the shallow water, and perched atop a tall white pine.

Both birds were aware of the other, their excellent eyesight actually enabling them to identify other eagles at distances up to three miles. The juvenile dove for a smallmouth bass, but missed. Instead of returning to its perch tree, the inquisitive juvenile soared towards Piercer. Not wanting to share that particular patch of water with the juvenile, Piercer dove directly at it. The juvenile did not fly and the adult smacked its head with a powerful wing beat. The youngster was dislodged from the oak and, after recovering its balance, began a retreat.

Although nearly five miles from his own nesting territory, Piercer felt the urge to drive the youngster from the area. As the sun dropped, a young cottontail rabbit ventured out from the protection of a blackberry thicket. Piercer focused his attention and when it sat upright and began nibbling on the tender blossoms of a clump of crimson clover he launched. With swept-back wings he plunged, leveling off five feet above the vegetation, he extended his feet. Shiny black talons struck the rabbit's rib cage, as the opposing talon of the hind toe penetrated its heart. Piercer lifted his two-pound capture and returned to a stout limb. Large clumps of soft fur drifted down on the breeze as the eagle enjoyed his meal.

Piercer spent summer days exploring sections of the Potomac River, often downriver from Moorefield. Fish were abundant, and seldom a day passed when he did not eat at least two. Much of August was spent along the Cacapon River, where wide, flat agricultural fields provided a variety of prey. Careless, young cottontail rabbits, gray squirrels, and an occasional groundhog yielded the rich, red meat preferred by many bald eagles.

As summer came to an end, human hunters made their appearance. Mourning doves were favorite targets and shotguns were favorite weapons. Some doves were killed but not retrieved by hunters. Others were crippled, but survived. One crippled mourning dove was discovered, killed, and consumed by Piercer. Almost every animal wounded by human hunters becomes a meal for some predator. Food is rarely wasted.

Talona and Piercer remained apart through September, each wandering into new river drainages. It was a relaxing time for Piercer. Food was abundant with multitudes of young-of-the-year that had left their mother and were now living independent lives for the first time.

Still separated from his mate, Piercer killed a groundhog, which had been wounded by a farmer. Tragically, for the eagle, the groundhog's body contained fragments of lead from the farmer's .22 bullet. Although the lead-core bullet had passed through the groundhog's shoulder, numerous, minute lead fragments remained in its muscles. Several dozen slivers of lead were swallowed by Piercer. The soft gray lead slowly disintegrated in his stomach due to the strong acids, and was subsequently absorbed into the eagle's bloodstream. From there it circulated throughout Piercer's body.

This was not Piercer's first experience with lead toxicity. In November, prior to mating with Talona, he had discovered the gut-pile of a white-tailed deer killed by human hunters. Lead fragments from a 30-30 rifle shell remained buried in the lungs and liver, and Piercer unwittingly consumed three grains of lead. Two particles were retained in his crop for five days and one in his stomach for three. Each pellet slowly disintegrated and tiny portions of lead entered his blood stream. His nervous and reproductive systems were affected, but he never exhibited the symptoms so indicative of lead toxicity.

Although his coordination was slightly compromised, his flying ability was only faintly impaired. Fortunately, fish were abundant and easy prey, and he slowly regained full hunting skills.

Piercer's recovery from the sub-lethal lead poisoning was somewhat unusual. One lead–core bullet from a deer rifle typically deposits hundreds of microscopic lead fragments – more than enough to result in the eventual death of a bald eagle.

Piercer's experience with the groundhog was not so fortunate. He became lethargic and began to lose balance and coordination in a little more than a week. He had difficulty maintaining a firm grip on a tree limb, and several times fell haplessly to the ground. Three days later, he could neither walk nor fly. Tremors shook his body, as he gasped for air. Sprawled on the forest floor with head outstretched and flat on the ground, he was completely helpless. A yearling black bear detected his scent and soon nothing remained of the eagle but feet and feathers.

In late October, when frost blanketed Canaan Valley with a silvery-white coating, Talona followed the Blackwater River upstream from Hendricks and dropped into the upper end of the drainage. Instinct had drawn her back. She soared over the Little Blackwater searching for Piercer. Failing to find her mate, she moved south to the Glade Run beaver-pond complex, but again had no luck finding her mate. A short flight brought her to Sand Run and the bulky nest where the two had spent so much time earlier that year. Perched on a familiar, talon-marred branch, she emitted a series of high-pitched screeches – each plaintiff cry aimed at announcing her presence to an unseen mate. Throughout November, she searched but Piercer never appeared. She remained the lone eagle in Canaan Valley.

The first week of December, Talona brought several dozen large sticks to her former nest. She strategically inserted them around the edge, elevating and strengthening the rim, instinctively preparing to protect eggs and eaglets during the upcoming nesting season. But she had no assistance – no partner – no Piercer. The new year arrived and Talona regularly visited her nest, even adding a few occasional sticks on sunny days.

THE NEW MATES

Talona remained in Canaan Valley until May, then she wandered west to the Tygart River. Summer was spent foraging along the Tygart from Grafton to Huttonsville. In October she returned to Canaan Valley where she resumed her fruitless search for Piercer.

Following unusually cold nights, Talona typically remained in her nighttime perch until the sun could warm the air. Such was the case one blue-sky day in late October. Nighttime temperatures had dropped to 20°F. On such days, energy was best conserved by remaining stationary. Talona stayed perched in one of her favorite black cherry trees while her eyes continuously scanned the surroundings. Around mid-morning, the sun's rays struck her. She changed her position several times, warming different parts of her body. By not flying, she burned significantly fewer calories.

As hunger pangs became too strong to ignore, she launched herself and a rising thermal carried her a thousand feet above the Valley floor. As she reached the height of Dolly Sods, at 4,000 foot-elevation, she scanned the relatively-flat plateau. Talona detected white-tailed deer browsing on viburnum shrubs and wild turkey scratching beneath small stands of black cherry trees but she ignored them. She also ignored a red-tailed hawk, in search of meadow voles.

The sun reflecting from the sharply contrasting black and white plumage of the eagle caught the attention of a group of hikers on Camp 70 Road. Although the majestic bird was easily visible, the close-up views provided by a pair of 8-power binoculars brought numerous exclamations of amazement. Ignoring the hikers, Talona focused on open stretches of water, searching for fish feeding near the surface.

As she approached the stretch of water where opposite hills pressed in on the river, Talona glimpsed a flash of gold. Dropping lower and tightening her flight circle, she initiated an attack. The fish was one of the golden trout released annually by the WVDNR.

When 70 feet from the fish, Talona entered attack mode. With neck outstretched, tail feathers spread, and wings swept backward, she dropped to 30 feet above the waters. At this point, her legs were thrust forward, with talons and toes spread wide. Her aim was true and, as she made contact with the water, talons of her right foot penetrated the back of the trout. Her grip tightened and she simultaneously initiated a series of wing flaps that carried her several feet above the water.

The hikers had lost sight of Talona when she dived but as she flapped skyward gripping the golden trout, applause and loud cries of amazement came from them. This rare sighting would be told and retold several times that night, as they enjoyed pizza and craft beer in Davis. It was a seminal experience that none of the hikers would ever forget.

With the arrival of November, and several heavy snowfalls, an immature bald eagle crossed high over the dam in Thomas and moved up the North Fork of the Blackwater River. The immature eagle was four years old, and lacked the white head and tail feathers characteristic of an adult.

In mid-November, the young male eagle spotted a large, high-soaring raptor nearly three miles distant. The raptor's black body stood out against a backdrop of scattered, puffy, cumulus clouds. And more importantly, its black body contrasted sharply with white head and tail when the background switched to bright blue. The majority of fish-eating birds are predominantly black and white, including gulls, terns, pelicans, and osprey. However, the young male eagle knew immediately he had discovered another bald eagle.

No other color combination is as visible at a distance as is black and white. Although not yet old enough to seek a mate, the male did prize the companionship of other bald eagles. Talona detected the young male within seconds. She did not alter her high-altitude soaring, but did shift her gaze to him. The male was soon soaring effortlessly behind her. With a slight repositioning, Talona climbed above the male and initiated a dive in his direction. For several minutes, the two eagles dived and circled, separated and closed. Although never touching, they were close enough to make eye contact. Talona identified the young eagle as a male, and he, in turn, identified her as a female.

Talona glided to one of her favorite perch trees. The male, hereafter known as Sylvus, was soon perched in the same tree. Within 30 minutes, he was sitting on the same horizontal limb as Talona and the two exchanged low-pitched screeches and attentive gazes. Although the female knew the male was not a likely suitor, she not only accepted his presence but strongly encouraged it. As the sun sunk, they perched three feet apart in one of Talona's favorite night roost trees.

Talona and Sylvus did not form a pair bond, but remained together in Canaan Valley until January, frequently perching on the same limb. As in the previous year, Talona added a few small branches to the rim of her nest during early winter. What little attachment Talona had to her nest ended abruptly in March. Following a meal of a largemouth bass, she descended to the ground and picked up a three-foot long fallen limb and flew towards the nest. When 25 yards away she was met by a male great-horned owl. Talona abruptly altered her flight. She was shocked to see a female great-horned owl sitting in the bowl she had so carefully created.

The pair of large owls had claimed the vacant nest in January. They had nested in a large birch tree the previous year, but that tree had fallen during a winter storm. The abandoned eagle nest met their needs, and in early March the female laid two dull white eggs. Talona paid no more visits to her former nest, and in April, two helpless, down-covered owlets made an appearance.

When temperatures dropped below freezing, and lakes and beaver ponds were solidly covered with ice, Sylvus departed. He had enjoyed Talona's company and there was a potential of the two eventually forming a breeding pair, but his fishing attempts in the Valley were consistently unsuccessful. Memories of more rewarding hunts pulled him eastward.

Sylvus had developed his hunting skills at a county landfill a short flight from the Potomac River. He had observed crows and vultures feeding at the landfill and duplicated their behavior. Numerous discarded food items from human kitchens and restaurants were available, but he soon discovered a more tasty meal – rats. Norway rats quickly built up a thriving population. The beady-eyed, scaly-tailed, gray-haired rodents were easy prey for any raptor still learning to hunt. Sylvus easily killed three to four per day.

The Norway rat population at the landfill had erupted the previous summer, and large amounts of an anticoagulant rodenticide were distributed around the landfill to control the pests. Hundreds of rats had been killed, but dozens more consumed sub-lethal doses and wandered awkwardly around the landfill for several days prior to dying. Unfortunately for Sylvus, these weakened individuals became easy prey.

Sylvus captured a rat which had consumed a small pellet soaked in an anticoagulant earlier that day. The anticoagulant passed from rat to bald eagle, and within a few hours Sylvus began to experience internal bleeding. Within 24 hours, hemorrhaging resulted in unclotted blood surrounding the heart and the liver. In two days, he became so weak and uncoordinated he had difficulty flying. Small amounts of blood seeped from his eyes and nostrils and he developed an intense thirst.

Sylvus survived two days and nights, but early the next morning, a dozer operator working at the landfill spotted him. Originally believing it to be a "buzzard," he lowered the dozer blade and began pushing a pile of soil towards him. The eagle flopped awkwardly and the operator realized it was not a vulture. Stopping his dozer, he climbed down to examine the bloody, dark-feathered bird. A phone call brought the office manager to the site, and Sylvus was soon wrapped in an old blanket and placed in a spacious cardboard box.

A call to a local raptor rehabilitation center brought the chief biologist to the landfill who initiated a thorough examination. The abundance of blood on the feathers suggested a gunshot. But an external exam produced no sign of gunshot and no broken bones. An exam of the bird's keel (breastbone) indicated the bird was suffering from starvation, and with emaciation had come dehydration. However, the rehabilitator had learned early in his career that providing water to a weakened raptor can lead to death. The liquid often enters the trachea, and from there the lungs – instead of passing down the throat. Aspiration and drowning are the result. Hydrating a physically-weakened bird in the field is usually only 20 percent successful.

An electrochemical field analysis of Sylvus' blood indicated he was not suffering from lead poisoning. Quickly returning the eagle to a carrying cage, he rushed back to the rehab center. Sylvus was given electrolytes and nutrients through esophageal intubation (a sterile plastic tube inserted through the esophagus and into the stomach). Unfortunately, internal bleeding resulting from the anticoagulant proved lethal. Sylvus died that night.

Another year passed, with no successful bald eagle nests in Canaan Valley.

Night Hooters and Other Nesting Intruders

Great-horned owls were not the only nocturnal raptor nesting in Canaan Valley that spring, although they were the first to lay eggs and begin incubating. Also in Canaan was another relatively large predator, the barred owl, plus two smaller species, the screech owl and saw-whet owl. A barred owl is approximately 80 percent the size of a great-horned owl, while screech and saw-whet owls are only about 20 percent. Wingspans range from 55 to 58 inches for the great-horned and 38 to 44 inches for the barred, down to 18 to 24 inches for the screech owl and 16 to 18 inches for the diminutive saw-whet.

Great-horned owls are capable of killing rabbits, skunks, and opossums, while barred owls typically kill smaller prey such as mice and flying squirrels, plus small rabbits and opossums. Screech owls concentrate on small mice, shrews, voles, and flying squirrels. The diet of saw-whet owls consists more heavily of mice and voles. Great-horned and barred owls frequently enjoy a meal of birds, while screech and saw-whet owls vary their diet by killing large insects.

None of the owls competed directly with Talona for food. Bald eagles never fed at night, while owls never fed during daylight. Thus, foods available to eagles were not available to owls. Rabbits were the lone exception. Cottontails feed primarily at night, although they will sit in the open at the edge of protective cover on sunny winter days. Competition was reduced even further because Talona focused her hunting forays around wetland areas. In contrast, great-horned owls hunted in forests and field edges. Bald eagle and great-horned owl confrontations occur when they nest too close to each other. Talona had even fewer interactions with barred owls. Both barred and great-horned owls are mortal enemies of crows, due mainly to an occasional owl swooping into a crow nest and flying off with a young crow.

While Talona had no conflicts with the small hawks – kestrel (sparrow hawk), sharp-shinned, and Cooper's – she did have interactions with the larger hawks. The carcass of a deer attracted eagles and hawks, but rarely both at the same time. Hawks would flee upon detecting bald eagles. Hawks, unlike crows or ravens or turkey vultures, rarely approached a feeding eagle.

Mobbing was the behavior that was the most common conflict between Talona and other birds. Crows initiated mobbing the most. A perching eagle would almost certainly attract a flock of crows. Most crows sat on limbs within 10 to 20 feet of Talona, while one or more individuals dived in reckless arcs at the eagle from overhead. Few crows actually touched the eagle, and almost never did Talona make an aggressive move towards them. Eagles were usually content to duck their heads to avoid pecks from a crow, and crows seemed to realize the placid eagle was no threat to them. Mobbing was done primarily to announce to all other crows in the general area that an eagle was present.

Mobbing typically involves a smaller bird "attacking" a larger bird. A pair of kestrels had a nest in a tree cavity about 90 yards from Sand Run Lake. When Talona soared overhead, the male kestrel flew to the same elevation as the eagle, and dived at it from behind, occasionally pecking at its tail or back. Kestrels were constantly on the lookout for an approaching eagle, fearing attacks on their nestlings.

The discovery of a screech owl inside a tree cavity during daylight hours by a chickadee or titmouse results in mass mobbing by a mixed flock of songbirds. The bravest will alight beside the cavity, stick its head inside, and erupt with a chorus of scolding calls. This further agitates the other "community mobbers" and dozens ultimately will let the owl know that it has been discovered. Such aggressive behavior is due, in part, to screech owls preying on nestlings of smaller songbirds.

Interactions between Talona and other birds at a deer carcass were fascinating. Crows typically arrived first, followed an hour or so later by a bald eagle or a hawk. When feeding crows spotted an incoming eagle, they set off a chorus of raucous cawing and flew wildly into the air. Their biggest fear was that the eagle would dive onto a crow and simultaneously drive it into the ground, held fast in the grip of its talons. Few crows ever survived an eagle's grasp. However, seldom did Talona ever make an attempt to capture a crow. Instead, she would simply flush the corvids, landing 10 to 12 feet from the carcass, and then clumsily hop to the deer.

Eagles are least impressive when moving on the ground. They have a comical form of locomotion, not really a walk and not really a hop. By moving one foot at a time, in moderately long hops, they awkwardly cover short distances. While doing so, their body seems to wobble. When needing to travel longer distances they utilize short flights.

Crows always moved aside for Talona to feed, but impatiently remained nearby. As the eagle ate, crows gradually eased in closer until several lurked within five feet of her. If Talona was feeding at one end of the carcass, one or two crows would eat at the other end. If plenty of flesh remained, Talona would be more tolerant than if bones had been picked clean. Eagles feeding on the ground are incredibly cautious, constantly looking around in all directions in search of an approaching predator.

When a family of crows was feeding with Talona, one individual would eventually attempt to drive the eagle from the carcass. The brazen crow stealthily approached the eagle from behind, often to within two feet. When Talona was preoccupied with ripping off a hunk of venison, the crow would dart forward, grab one of her tail feathers and jerk backwards. Talona would instantly make a short jump towards the crow, but never inflicted injury. Crows never drove Talona from a carcass, and she never caught a crow.

A hawk feeding at a carcass when Talona approached would

immediately fly away until the eagle left. In contrast, hawks and crows frequently fed together, although crows were more aggressive towards comparably-sized raptors than they were towards an eagle. Not only would crows pull the tail feathers of a hawk, but they would fly onto its back and sink their claws into its flesh. Hawks flew aggressively at the annoying crows, but rarely caught one.

Fatal interactions occur only when eagles fly into a nest and remove a young hawk or crow. This is rare, with eagles much less likely to remove young from a nest than are great-horned owls. Talona's most serious conflicts with birds were those involving other eagles. Such events typically occurred in winter, when food was scarce and competition was amplified. Eagles also felt the urge to defend a breeding territory during winter, even though they had no mate and no nest.

In January 2019, most bodies of water had frozen solid, making it extremely difficult for Talona to capture fish. The annual WVDNR hunting season for deer had since ended. The carcasses and gut piles had been totally consumed. Life was tough for an eagle in Canaan Valley.

On this January day, as luck would have it, Talona was rewarded by the sounds of feeding ravens. Moments later, she was again perched atop a deer carcass. Nearly 20 minutes later Talona saw 200 yards distant another eagle, but continued feeding. When 60 yards away she suspected it was not a bald eagle, and stopped feeding. As the bird dived towards Talona her instincts were confirmed; it was a golden eagle.

Bald eagles and golden eagles are approximately the same size. Immature bald eagles do not obtain the white head and tail until mature, at five to six years of age. They have noticeable white on their wing linings, while golden eagles have white at the base of their tail and small white patches in their flight feathers, resulting in the two species bearing a close resemblance.

Humans are challenged to distinguish between an immature bald eagle and an adult golden eagle – unless light conditions are optimal. At a close distance however, the golden yellow, unfeathered legs and oversized, bright-yellow beak provide distinguishing characteristics for most bald eagles. Feathered brown legs, dark brown beak, and relatively small beak and head confirmed to Talona that the approaching eagle was an immature golden.

Talona sprung into the air and interrupted the flight of the approaching eagle. She had no intention of sharing. The immature eagle was four years old, and would be attaining its golden neck feathers later that year. Flaring its wings, it extended its feet and talons as far forward as possible, in preparation for Talona's impact. They clasped toes and talons, and tumbled awkwardly to the ground. With more strength and experience in fighting, Talona was soon atop the younger bird. A sharp bite to one of its flapping wings inflicted serious pain, and the immature attempted to break free. Talona tightened her grip, and struck again at the flailing eagle's other wing. As the immature pulled one foot free, Talona released her grip and lunged at the immature which jumped into the air and escaped. When it flew out of sight, Talona returned to her meal.

As the fight had been occurring, multiple, motion-activated trail cameras were filming the action. This particular baited site was one of hundreds running the length of the Central and Southern Appalachians. Several state and federal wildlife agencies were cooperating on a study aimed at understanding golden eagle migration patterns. The majority of those golden eagles living east of the Rocky Mountains nest in Quebec, then migrate south through the Appalachians to their wintering grounds. Birds from Quebec cross into New York, south through Pennsylvania, and down the spine of the Appalachians, with many roughly following the Virginia-West Virginia state line. This cooperative study involved dumping deer carcasses, capturing eagles with rocket nets, attaching telemetry units, and tracking their travels to and from nesting sites.

The wildlife biologists wanted to capture and tag only golden eagles. If Talona filled her crop that afternoon and allowed the immature golden to come to the carcass, the biologists would activate the rocket net. If captured, a transmitter would be attached and the bird would contribute to our knowledge of golden eagle migration.

By late February, biologists had captured their annual quota at that site and stopped baiting and trapping. With no more deer carcasses available at the various tagging locations, Talona returned to Canaan Valley in March.

MOUNT STORM LAKE

Four miles east of the northern end of Canaan Valley lay Mount Storm Lake. Constructed in 1965 to provide cooling water for a coal-fired power plant, this 1,200-acre reservoir was created by damming the Stony River. Surrounded by forested habitat on the west and south, and supporting large fish populations, the lake provided better habitat for bald eagles than did Canaan Valley. Because warm water was recirculated as a critical element of burning coal to produce electricity, that portion of the lake in close proximity to the physical plant remained free of ice in winter. Although the upper reaches of the lake froze in winter, it still provided excellent fishing for bald eagles.

A pair of bald eagles moved into the area from the Potomac River in 2008, and a nest was constructed along the western edge of the lake in December 2009. That nest successfully fledged eaglets in 2010 and 2011, and every spring through 2021. Talona occasionally flew from Canaan Valley to Mount Storm, but was driven away by the pair, especially when eggs or eaglets were present. Talona occasionally searched its shoreline for fish during summer months, but concentrated on the upper shorelines further away from the successful nest. The nesting pair tolerated her presence during summer, but as winter approached she was constantly driven away.

Over 100 homes were located at Mount Storm Lake. Charles Alvin and his wife, Julie had a home here. The Alvins had lived in Cumberland, Maryland, approximately 40 miles away. A few years prior to Charles' retirement, the couple had bought land, and spent five years building their retirement home. The house was less than 100 yards from the lake, with expansive picture windows and adjacent deck providing spectacular year-round views.

The Alvins spent several hours each day watching wildlife. Feeders attracted a variety of birds. Hummingbirds entertained them during summer months, while blue jays, cardinals, chickadees, juncos, gold finches, grosbeaks, titmice, and woodpeckers provided winter excitement.

Osprey appeared frequently, as did the lake's pair of bald eagles. However, the eagles spent most of their time near their nest over a mile away. Three hundred yards from the house was a small grove of mature black cherry trees, and a few days each year an adult eagle was spotted here.

Charles bought a variable power (15X-60X) Bausch & Lomb Zoom 60 mm Telescope, and spent hours observing the eagles. When two birds sat together he took great satisfaction in identifying their sex. As with all eagles, the female was noticeably larger than the male, but not enough that Charles could tell the difference when only one bird was present.

The Alvins had an outdoor microphone which broadcast into their living room. It was exceptionally sensitive, and could pick up not only the vocalizations of birds at their feeders, but the screeches of an eagle several hundred yards away.

Julie Alvin had read every book on bald eagles she could find, and knew bald eagle nests were often no more than one-half mile apart. Charles and Julie wondered if it was possible to have a second nest on the lake. Julie became quite excited reading about a study in Maine, which determined that artificial feeding would result in an increase of nesting eagles. Wildlife biologists had placed deer carcasses in areas not utilized by nesting eagles, and several of the sites attracted eagles, and eventually nests. Could they attract a second pair of eagles if they provided supplemental foods, Julie wondered?

Charles and Julie typically drove to Moorefield each week to shop.

Most of their drive was along the relatively new, four-lane Corridor H (U.S. Route 48). On many trips they spotted the carcass of a road-killed deer, as well as carcasses of groundhogs, opossums, and raccoons. As cold weather returned, and carcasses remained relatively "fresh" Charles began salvaging those that did not smell too badly. He carried garbage bags and sunflower seed bags in their Jeep. Groundhogs, opossums, and raccoons were retrieved intact and stowed in a plastic bag and then in a heavy sunflower seed bag. A plastic tie sealed the bag and prevented any – or at least most – unpleasant odors from escaping into their Jeep.

Julie was adamant in not wanting a dead deer in the rear of their Jeep as many were bloody and would seep into the 4 X 4's upholstery. Charles separated each shoulder and leg from the carcass with a butcher knife. Beginning at the "armpit" he found it easy to slice through the thin skin. A continuous cut around the top of the shoulder resulted in the shoulder/ leg falling loose into an awaiting sack. Each shoulder blade was "free-floating" and the removal of shoulder/leg required no cutting of bones. The entire operation required less than 15 minutes.

Once home, Charles carried the meat to a grassy spot 20 feet from the shoreline and directly down from the black cherry trees. Then the waiting began. Crows typically were the first to discover the food.

The first eagle appeared at the "road-kill" site in late September and fed on a raccoon carcass. The first offering of deer shoulders, around 11 a.m. on October 15, attracted the crows within an hour. At 4 p.m. a bald eagle swooped down. The crows retreated to the other leg and fed until dusk. With daylight fast fading, eagle and crows headed for their nighttime roost.

Vociferous crows awakened Charles the next morning at dawn. He hurried to his spotting scope and saw two bald eagles feeding – one on each deer leg. Annoyed crows remained several feet away.

The Alvins continued to deposit road-kills through the middle of November and made detailed records of the behaviors of crows, eagles, and an occasional raven. Road-kills were not discovered every week, resulting in the Alvins being entertained only sporadically.

Charles learned of a deer processing facility a few miles north of Moorefield. Heads, leg bones, backbones, and rib cages were dumped into an open-topped trailer. The trailer was hauled to a county landfill where the contents were dumped and covered with soil by bulldozers. Operators were glad to have the Alvins take all the deer they could haul. Their Jeep was typically filled with three large garbage bags, plus their groceries each week.

During archery season (the first three weeks of November), when only occasional deer were being harvested, the deer processing facility became an unreliable supply of carcasses. However, during the two-week deer gun season at the end of November, their trailer was overflowing. Doe season and the primitive weapons season in December and early January brought dozens of deer carcasses to the processing plant. At those times, the Alvins hauled home four large black garbage bags. The rib cages were hung in an outside storage shed, to be saved for later, but four or five large neck bones were immediately left at the feed site.

At the end of deer hunting season, the Alvins discovered a beef butchering facility near Petersburg, and were overjoyed to learn they could obtain a garbage bag full of beef or pork backbones every week. They quickly learned that eagles and crows enjoyed beef and pork just as well as they did venison.

Talona began making daily trips to Mt. Storm Lake in late November and through December. Talona learned to avoid the existing eagle pair, and fly directly to the eastern side of the lake to study the feeding site from a mile away.

In early January, with nesting season approaching, the eagle pair became especially aggressive towards Talona. Their attacks were so fierce that she halted all visits to the lake and her days were restricted to Canaan Valley. Among her favorite sites was the upper end of Sand Run Lake. The shallow, upstream end of this elongated body of water contained an active beaver pond, an extensive marsh, and several long stretches where ice rarely formed. When the totality of that body of water was ice-covered, Talona focused her foraging on the constant-flowing Blackwater River and its Sand Run tributary. During even the coldest spells, Talona succeeded in capturing at least one fish every couple days.

A four-year old juvenile bald eagle had appeared in Canaan Valley in late-December and was witnessed by Talona. He displayed none of the behaviors that aroused her own mating instincts, and she barely tolerated him. With her former nest now defended by the pair of great-horned owls, she was drawn to another site, this one high on the hillside overlooking the lower end of Sand Run. She carried several sticks into the forks of a black cherry tree and instinctively began constructing a nest. However, with no male available she abandoned the project.

And so, January 2020 passed with no mate for Talona. No nest was built, no eggs were laid, and no eaglets were fledged in Canaan Valley that spring – another unproductive year.

MOUNT STORM CONTROVERSY

The DNR had been scheduled to scatter old Christmas trees here in late February to benefit fish. Unfortunately, the Mt. Storm Power Station was rebuilding their major boat-loading ramp, and the fisheries biologists needed to ascertain whether they could back a boat trailer of Christmas trees down the ramp and into the lake.

While passing in front of the Alvin's house in their Jon boat, the biologists spotted two bald eagles feeding on the shore. An examination revealed a small pile of rib cages and backbones, not dead fish as they had expected. A repeat visit two weeks later again revealed two feeding bald eagles. And, again they discovered deer rib cages. Eventually word reached a DNR game warden, and a week later he mentioned the incident to a Special Agent with the U.S. Fish and Wildlife Service (USFWS).

After a quick examination of the shoreline, the agents were knocking on the Alvin's door. The Alvins explained that they were simply trying to attract bald eagles for close-up observation and photographs. When the federal agent explained that they were breaking federal law, Julie grew a little defensive.

She asked for a copy of the law, and then countered, "You wardens should be trying to catch the duck hunters who shoot out of season and long after sundown when shooting hours end. We're just feeding hungry wildlife and aren't hurting anything."

The agent patiently explained, "When bald eagles concentrate at a food source, birds often fight and juveniles might be injured. It is illegal, under federal law, to disturb or harass an eagle. Feeding has been interpreted by federal judges as disturbing their normal behavior." He attempted to pacify Julie by showing her a copy on his phone.

Julie brusquely responded, "I can't read that small print. You need to give me a printed copy, with large letters, so I can read it carefully."

Similarly put off, Charles added, "Explain to me why it's legal to feed songbirds, but not legal to feed eagles! If I'm harming eagles, then I'm certainly harming the cardinals and chickadees, the grosbeaks and blue jays, and the titmice and woodpeckers. What about feeding wild turkeys? Many of our neighbors put out shelled corn for turkeys. Is that illegal?"

Julie interjected, "We read in the newspaper about wildlife biologists dumping deer carcasses to trap and tag golden eagles. Why don't you go arrest them?"

Unperturbed, the federal agent responded, "I'll get you a printed copy of the law and let you read all the details. Meantime, you need to quit putting out meat for eagles. Incidentally, the law for feeding bald eagles provides for a fine of $5,000 per incident, imprisonment for one year, or both."

That information totally shocked the Alvins, and with no further comment, Charles closed the door. Julie wanted to have the last word, and called through the door, "Do you really believe we are doing any harm to the eagles?"

The Alvins received a thick packet the following week. Julie spent the better part of three days reading through the material, and finally conceded that indeed it might be illegal to directly feed bald eagles.

The Alvins ceased the feeding but Charles wanted to somehow continue. He proposed they use their small fishing boat to haul bones to a hidden cove about one mile away. He reasoned that eagles would still be attracted to the meat, and they might build a nest somewhere on the east side of the lake.

Julie had another idea. She suggested they begin harvesting large numbers of fish, especially large channel catfish. "Let's set out five or ten trotlines, buy a small chest freezer, and collect lots of big catfish. We can scatter them at various places back a short distance from the shore, so the feeding eagles would not be readily seen from a boat. We don't need to use beef, pork, or deer bones."

Charles stubbornly commented, "I'm certain it is legal to put out bait for coyotes. I've been wanting to buy a game camera to get some good pictures of coyotes, or bobcats, or even a mountain lion."

The next day Charles ordered four trail cameras. Each was camouflaged, motion-activated, and transmitted images to his smartphone. After several weeks of trials, he was confident he could get good images of a coyote or bobcat – or even a bald eagle – if one should carelessly pass in front of a camera.

He "baited" each camera with a couple pig leg bones. Charles knew that crows cache dozens, if not hundreds, of small bits of flesh a short distance from the carcass. Once they had eaten their fill, he had watched them fly 20 to 50 yards and poke the food deep into the grass. Weeks or months later they would return to the cached meat and either eat it or carry it to hungry youngsters in their nest. He reasoned the site was far enough from their home for plausible deniability, should his actions be detected.

The first night of baiting was a failure. The bones were carried off, but Charles had decided not to activate the flash and obtained no images of the thief. The next night he drove a small wooden stake more than two feet into the ground, and secured several bones with baling twine. He did not want to use rope or wire because he feared it would frighten away eagles. The bones were stolen again that night. The next day, Charles drilled a hole through the end of each leg bone, and tied a piece of clothesline wire to the wooden stake. He was convinced this setup would most likely prevent a coyote from hauling it off, but he worried the clothesline wire was so shiny it might frighten off an eagle. Although tempted to activate the flash to reveal the bone thief, he was more concerned about getting good images of feeding bald eagles.

Dozens of images of feeding crows were transmitted to his cellphone during the next two days, but no eagles. Charles continued baiting the site throughout March, but got no eagle pictures.

On pleasant days in March, Charles and Julie began taking their fishing boat for leisurely cruises around the lake. They knew the location of the bald eagle nest from previous years, and were pleased to discover an adult sitting on a limb about 20 feet from the nest. Although the second adult was rarely visible from their boat, it would occasionally stand in the nest and its white head would come into view.

Unbeknownst to the humans, the female had laid three eggs during the second week of February. As the weeks passed, as many as four other fishing boats with eagle watchers often anchored along the shoreline. As she and Charles studied the nest, Julie commented, "If the game wardens were really concerned about protecting the eagles they wouldn't allow so many boats to anchor so close to the nest. It seems to me there is considerably more harassment taking place here than at our feeding station."

The Alvins saw no bald eagles near their house when eaglets were in the nest. An occasional osprey circled the lake, and the Alvins regularly studied a tree where ospreys often made a meal of a fish. Intrigued, in April Charles built a 20-foot tall nest platform for the fish hawks. To his disappointment, none used it that summer. The platform was situated about 20 feet from the shoreline, and was, however, frequently used by red-winged blackbirds, crows, kestrels, and a red-shouldered hawk.

While monitoring the eagle nest from their fishing boat in June, Julie discovered one of the juvenile eagles sitting in a tree. The other two nestling eaglets were sitting on the rim of the nest. The Alvins remained in the area for several hours, during which time the adults brought fish to the two nestlings, but none to the fledgling perched out of the nest.

Julie commented, "I'd like to put out food for the fledgling eagles later this month. I read that they have a difficult time learning to capture fish, and the parents provide them with almost no training. Some starve to death before they are able to provide for themselves."

In early July Charles loaded his ATV with trail cameras plus a dozen pig leg bones, and motored to the secluded cove. He had obtained permission from a neighbor to pass through his locked gate and follow an ATV trail to the cove. He sincerely doubted the game warden would be searching the lake for scavenging crows or vultures.

Charles continued his trail camera surveys through July. A family of coyotes, several red foxes, a bobcat, a black bear, and dozens of crows, ravens, and vultures visited the site. But, no eagles. In August he retrieved his game cameras, resolving to renew his surveys in December. Late autumn and early winter were the best times to attract bald eagles to a new site, which was the Alvin's major goal.

STRONG CIRCUMSTANTIAL EVIDENCE

Talona returned to Canaan Valley from the Tygart River in October 2021. Her main objective was to find other bald eagles. Discovering none, she visited her former nest. The great-horned owls had reared another clutch of owlets, and the nest appeared to be in excellent condition.

One crisp autumn morning, Talona spotted a raptor soaring over Dolly Sods. She caught a thermal and rode it to 4,000 feet. Although more than a mile away, she quickly identified it as a bald eagle. There was no mistaking the white head and tail. However, a face-to-face meeting was required to see if it was a male. Both eagles were curious about the other, but were reluctant to approach too closely.

Talona dropped low over the Sods, and alighted on a high branch. As midday shadows were at their minimum, the other eagle returned to the air and soared in Talona's direction.

A few friendly aerial circles a hundred yards above Talona convinced both eagles they had nothing to fear from an encounter. The second eagle landed less than 20 yards from Talona. Talona emitted a shrill screech, but remained in her own spruce. Using extreme caution, she thoroughly examined the other eagle. Although no distinct identifying features revealed its sex, within minutes Talona knew it was a male. Timbre, as the male shall hereafter be named, knew Talona was a female too.

During the next two weeks the two perched, soared, and fed together. By the end of November, a preliminary pair bond had formed. The male was six years old, mature enough to complete all the duties required of a reproducing mature eagle. He had hatched along the Cheat River, in Pennsylvania, a short distance north of Cheat Lake Dam.

I first spotted the two eagles in November 2021, sitting on a black cherry tree along Sand Run. That same day, I spotted them side-by-side feeding on a deer carcass.

On December 1, I observed two eagles, assumed to be Talona and Timbre, sitting within eight feet of one another in a black cherry tree. With no visible signal, the obviously larger female departed the tree, followed almost immediately by the male. Timbre followed 10 to 15 feet behind, as the two performed an elaborate courtship flight. Moving in large circles, 300 feet above the ground, the pair enjoyed ten minutes of rapid, tandem flight.

The next day Timbre was sitting in the same tree when 2,000 feet above, flew a flock of about 300 whistling swans. Timbre recognized their broken "V" formation and all-white plumage, but showed only faint interest. The swans had departed their nesting grounds in Canada and were headed for wintering grounds along the Chesapeake Bay. Rarely did they land in Canaan Valley, preferring to make their fall migration trip from Lake Erie to Chesapeake Bay a non-stop journey. Only their unique high-pitched honking calls informed humans and other wildlife of their passage.

With constant head swiveling, Timbre searched for potential prey – or competing bald eagles. He focused his attention on Talona, as she flew in from the south. With little effort she adjusted her flight and landed softly two feet from Timbre. Then she sidled close and gently brushed her shoulder against his. Her overture was followed by bending her head backward, stretching her beak towards the sky, and emitting several low screeches. Although her calls would not be described as sensuous by humans, apparently they were interpreted as such by Timbre. In response, he likewise bent his head backward and stretched his beak to the sky, echoing Talona's call.

This intimate behavior was followed by the two birds gently clacking their beaks together while holding mouths open. Their courtship continued for 12 minutes, at which time Talona again pushed gently against Timbre with her shoulder. The male eagle held firmly, but did not visibly respond in any other manner. Five more minutes of foreplay followed, and most humans might have concluded that copulation would ensue. Talona performed another soft shoulder push, but when Timbre made no satisfactory response she launched herself towards a deer carcass 200 yards away.

A short time later, Timbre landed near Talona, and began sharing a deer dinner. One week later, I discovered them on a partially-submerged log on the lake. Each would bend over, dip its beak into the water, raise its head to swallow, and next scan the surroundings for anything suspicious. Then the process was repeated. I concluded the birds were definitely a "dedicated" pair.

Two days later, I spotted them feeding on a nearly-meatless deer carcass. They fed within a foot of one another, obviously comfortable with each other's company. Following the meal, the Talona made slow circles over the lake and within five minutes Timbre joined her. They flew in close tandem. The aerial courtship was exciting to watch, especially when they locked talons and plunged earthward. When only 70 or 80 feet above the water they disengaged, and continued their slow, wide circles.

Once again, my anticipation erupted to high levels as I envisioned a bald eagle nest in Canaan Valley. It had been five years since I discovered the active, but later abandoned, nest. In 2020, I saw adult bald eagles every month except September and November. The next year, I sighted adult eagles monthly, January through May. My hopes of finding an active nest were shattered, however, during February and March of 2021, when I spotted the pair sitting together in a black cherry tree. Eggs and newly-hatched eaglets are never left alone in a nest during February and March. Another breeding season thus passed, and my frustration continued. Whether the eagles were also frustrated could not be determined.

In 2020 and 2021, I quizzed cyclists and hikers about sightings of a bald eagle nest. In addition, I also contacted Canaan Valley National Wildlife Refuge and Canaan Valley State Park but received no reports of a pair of bald eagles.

Although I did not really consider myself old, I was, in fact, approaching my 85th birthday, and finding a successful bald eagle nest in Canaan Valley was at the top of my bucket list. How many more years could I trudge through the bogs and alder thickets? I wanted Canaan Valley to have an eagle nest, and I wanted to be the person who discovered it.

I have watched birds most of my life. In my opinion, there is no bird in North America as majestic as a mature bald eagle – in size, in coloration, in weapons, and in facial expressions. The six-foot wingspan is matched only by that of the golden eagle and the great-blue heron. Even more evident is the black and white coloration of an adult bald eagle, which can be identified at a greater distance than can that of any other animal. Glaring eyes, bright-yellow hooked beak, and shiny black talons accentuate its striking appearance.

So it was with elation that I watched a pair of adult eagles feeding on a deer carcass the first week of 2022. Their appearance was a good sign. However, on January 7, I spotted three adult bald eagles sitting together in a black cherry tree. That was not a good sign. If two of the birds were indeed a pair and had initiated nest construction, they would not tolerate the presence of another adult. My optimism received a boost just before dark the next day when I spotted two eagles sitting only six feet apart. I conducted a search the next evening, and much to my surprise and joy, there were again two adult eagles sitting side-by-side in the same black cherry tree. There had to be a nest nearby, I surmised.

A few days later, Talona sailed effortlessly to Sand Run Lake, and alighted in an 80-foot black cherry tree. The tree was one of her favorites, allowing her a clear view of a small cove.

The tree was also one of my personal favorites. It was directly downhill from my cabin, about 150 yards distant, and provided countless

opportunities for me to study the courtship of the pair of bald eagles.
I was sitting near my wood stove, enjoying oatmeal and hot tea when
Talona arrived.

Her attention was drawn to another bald eagle approaching from the
south. When 400 yards away, she recognized Timbre, and called to him.
He had already spotted her and headed in her direction. Her inviting
call was most welcome. The male dropped low over the shoreline, and
suddenly dropped to the ground in a large patch of dried grass. After a
couple characteristic eagle-hops, he grasped a large clump of dried grass
and sprang into the air. He alighted beside Talona, and they exchanged
greetings, and Talona edged closer to Timbre. When within six inches she
halted and stretched her head skyward.

I moved to my spotting scope, and increased the variable power
to 40X – providing an excellent, close-up view of the two eagles. I was
pleased to see they were still a dedicated pair, and enjoying each other's
company. I fully expected to see courtship, but that was not to be the case
that morning. Talona studied the handful of dried grass, and even pulled
off a few of the stems. I concluded that Timbre had brought his mate a
gift of grass, just as I had brought a handful of wild flowers to an attractive
young woman during my own courtship – many decades earlier.

Courtship often follows a bumpy, winding path, especially for bald
eagles. Although Timbre probably expected a little positive reinforcement
from Talona, he was disappointed to see her fly away. A few minutes later,
he released his clump of grass, and stayed for nearly 30 minutes.

On January 14, I was again thrilled to spot them feeding together.
I concluded they were likely a mated pair. On January 16, I became
positively convinced they were a mated pair, and that a nest definitely
existed nearby. I had discovered a dead 30 pound grass carp stretched out
on a small gravel bar. Only a small portion of the fish had been eaten.
I carried the carp, still relatively fresh, to a floating bog bordering the
lake that was visible from my cabin and was covered with low-growing
vegetation. Sphagnum moss and sprawling beds of cranberries provided

excellent 360⁰ visibility for a feeding bald eagle. This mattered because super-wary bald eagles typically avoid feeding in areas dominated by shrubs.

Sand Run Lake and my cabin lay in "Old Timberline," a gated vacation home community of nearly 2,700 acres with 366 homes. Fifty-five of the homes were owned by permanent residents, while the remainder were owned by persons such as myself, who were part-time residents.

Every summer, I caught hundreds of bluegill from Sand Run Lake while fishing from a canoe, and routinely scattered their remains on the bog after fileting my catch. I hoped to attract a river otter, although none had ever been sighted in Canaan Valley. The fish carcasses typically were scavenged instead by mink, raccoons, coyotes, and foxes, plus crows, vultures, and an occasional bald eagle. In addition, I always threw a few bluegill carcasses into the lake to feed the ever-hungry snapping turtles.

The morning after I moved the grass carp carcass I was awakened by the local crow family. My wildlife microphone picked up the crows' conversation and broadcast it through a small speaker in my bedroom. I kept a spotting scope set up and a quick examination revealed the carp carcass. It had survived the night – without being hauled off by one of the resident carnivores. Although coyotes, foxes, and raccoons relished fish, the carp must have been too large for them to haul away.

About an hour later, while eating my oatmeal, I watched an eagle soar in from the upper end of the lake. Although it was impossible for me to identify the eagle's gender, an amazing event some 20 minutes later enabled me to make a positive determination. The lone bird twice circled low over the carp carcass. As the eagle landed a few feet from the carp, the crows scattered, although one especially brave individual remained within six feet of the eagle. Several short hops brought the eagle to the carp.

The eagle had been feeding for 20 minutes when I spotted a second bald eagle gliding in from the same direction as the first had. That eagle made a small semi-circle over the feeding eagle, about eight feet overhead, and – much to my surprise – landed directly atop the feeding eagle. Never had I witnessed such action by any raptor. One bird never lands directly atop another – unless it is a predator landing atop a prey.

I believed one eagle was attacking the other, but I could not have been more wrong. While eagle number one braced itself, the second eagle tenderly braced its talons onto the back of the first eagle. Copulation immediately followed, allowing me to identify eagle number one as a female (Talona) and the second eagle as a male (Timbre). What a great morning to be a bald eagle, and what a memorable morning to be a wildlife biologist.

The two eagles fed on the carp for 40 minutes, then flew towards the prominent black cherry tree. I spent several days searching for a nest, but concluded there wasn't one because they are very distinct, especially in winter.

During the week of January 17, I discovered the carcass of a coyote-killed deer in a small alder thicket. I hauled the half-eaten carcass to the floating bog where I had placed the dead carp. Three days later, the eagles discovered the carcass. I assumed this was the same pair I had observed copulating atop the carp the previous week. They again flew south after their fill of venison. However, because the upper end of the lake was not visible from my cabin, I could not identify where the eagles were roosting.

To solve this mystery I sat opposite the southeastern end of the lake. I wore camouflage clothing and was hidden by numerous beech saplings. I believed the eagles would not see me as they flew in or out. I wore a thick wool toboggan, insulated gloves, and insulated boots, coveralls over insulated underwear and wool pants. A small foam cushion and hand warmers provided some small amount of comfort as I sat for nearly three hours that first morning.

I had arrived at my observation post around 9 a.m., knowing eagles typically arrived at the deer carcass around 9:30 a.m. It was 20°F, but rays of the morning sun provided a little warmth. At 9:50 a.m. I spotted a lone eagle soaring towards the deer carcass. As usual, it made two circles over the deer carcass, before dropping to the ground. Landing 12 feet from the carcass, it awkwardly hopped to breakfast. The presence of crows eliminated any fears the eagle might have had about present danger. If a coyote had been lurking nearby, the crows would have discovered it, and remained a safe distance away. A small flock of crows has a much better chance of spotting a predator than does a single eagle.

Bald eagles efficiently "butcher" the carcass of a deer or other animal. They hop atop the carcass, sink their talons into the hide to establish a firm anchor, and begin cutting and tearing small chunks of flesh. These are swallowed whole, with no chewing or hesitation. With no teeth, the sharp edge of their beak provides their only cutting instrument. Flesh, small bones, and hair pass into the crop, and eventually from there into the gizzard. Flesh is digested from bones, hair, and other indigestible components and moves down into the stomach.

Materials that cannot be digested, such as hair and bones, are regurgitated as pellets of about two by three inches in size. An adult eagle can eat approximately one pound in 30 to 40 minutes. After eating they typically drink, fly off to a tree, then sit, sleep, and digest their meal. Although they typically eat once per day, it is not unusual for them to go two days without eating.

The lone eagle I watched fed about 30 minutes, then hopped to the water's edge for a drink. It took six beakfuls of near-freezing water before flying off. Although I did not see exactly where it landed, I saw the general area where it headed.

Nearly an hour later, another adult eagle appeared from the south and soared to the deer carcass. The second eagle ate then followed the same return route as the first. I was quite pleased with my survey, and grew convinced the eagles were nesting around the south end of Sand Run Lake.

The following week, as dusk settled, I eased my way along the lakeshore to a point where I had a clear view of where the eagles had flown the previous week. I was rewarded with a view of two eagles sitting together about five feet apart. Two nights later, I again spotted the eagles on the same limb. What pleasure and what promise! Three days later, I conducted a thorough ground search, and discovered four pellets regurgitated by the eagles. The largest, at two by three inches, was a mass of soft white hair. The others were slightly smaller, and consisted of both brown and white hairs.

At the close of January I discovered another deer carcass along a tributary of Sand Run. Coyotes had opened the stomach cavity and partially disemboweled it. I pulled out the stomach and intestines, but left the kidneys, liver, lungs, and heart inside the rib cage. I dragged the carcass to the floating bog and retreated to my cabin.

I observed two adult eagles feeding together at the deer carcass two days later (January 26 and 27) and again on February 4. However, on February 17 and February 18 only single, solitary bald eagles were observed feeding and perching. The presence of single adult eagles in February was promising. If the pair had eggs in the nest, it would be highly unusual for both to be away from the nest at the same time.

On March 10, I watched an eagle feed on a raccoon then fly off towards the south. Fifteen minutes later, an eagle flew in from the south. There was no way the two were the same eagle. I was convinced they were a mated pair.

Eggs usually are laid sometime the second or third week of February, and the adults would have incubated them for the next five weeks — hatching occurring around the third week of March.

During that three-day period when I spotted individual eagles feeding, I again conducted evening vigils. However, I detected no eagles in the black cherry stand and my confidence about a nest in those woods was slightly shaken.

I had been watching a live video feed of an eagle nest on the Monongahela River near Pittsburgh, and knew the Pennsylvania female had laid her eggs the second week of February. Canaan Valley eagles should have been on a similar schedule.

Although I had observed the Canaan eagles throughout February and the first week of March, I did not make an intensive search to locate a nest. There was no urgency, as I was convinced they were a mated pair. An on-foot search through the scattered patches of woods could frighten them and result in nest abandonment. Although quite curious, I convinced myself to continue observing from my cabin. Once a female begins incubating, the male delivers food to the nest. And after the eggs hatch, the transporting of fish to the nest becomes a daily requirement. Of special importance to my search, I knew bald eagles will not transport chunks of flesh torn from a carcass back to their nest. Only entire carcasses are transported.

During the week of March 15, I changed my strategy. Afternoon temperatures had risen into the 70s and had dropped below freezing on only one night. I kept several dozen half-gallon milk cartons with bluegill heads, skeletons, and tails in my deep freeze. I had caught them in summer for trapping snapping turtles after they emerged from hibernation. Now I would put them to better use. I thawed two containers, woke the next morning at daylight, and trudged to the floating bog. My jaunt was highlighted by the dazzling sight of Venus, along with a significantly less bright Mars low in the eastern sky.

I placed four of the largest fish skeletons on the surface of the bog, two feet from the water's edge. The remaining bluegill skeletons were carefully scattered in three to five inch deep water, within two feet of the shoreline. I hoped crows would not wade into water to retrieve them and most would remain available for an observant bald eagle. Returning to my cabin, I crawled back into bed for a while.

The raucous cawing of crows was broadcast into my bedroom and awakened me from a pleasant sleep, just minutes before the sun became visible. I observed five crows pecking at the largest bluegill on the bog. A short time later, two crows discovered the bluegill in the lake, but were reluctant to wade into the water. One of the braver ones poked at a carcass I had dropped close to land, and managed to drag it onto shore. At least

14 carcasses probably remained in the water.

My observation done, I built a fire in my woodstove. While eating breakfast, a bald eagle flew in from the south. It quickly discovered the fish. After gleaning the remaining flesh, it picked up a large bluegill head and flew low over the water towards the south.

Nearly an hour later, an adult bald eagle circled twice over the bluegill skeletons and landed beside three large heads. I was surprised to see the eagle pick up a head with its beak, and head south. I had never observed an eagle carrying anything in its beak. An eagle's beak enables it to extract and hold small food items for nestling eaglets. It is also strong enough to rip apart prey animals. The tip of the pointed beak has a prominent curve that permits the bird to intricately remove tidbits of flesh at joints where two bones meet.

While the beak of an eagle somewhat resembles the prehensile fingers of a mammal, the feet are a more marvelous tool. Few birds use their feet for tasks other than perching. A bald eagle uses its feet for perching securely during severe winds, for transporting sticks and other nest materials, for killing and transporting prey, for fighting competitors, for turning a carcass, and for dragging a carcass a short distance. Rough pads cover the soles of both feet, enabling the eagle to grasp slippery, squirming fish. An eagle foot consists of four muscular toes, three facing forward and one (the hallux) facing to the rear.

I believed the bluegills were visible from the patch of black cherry trees where I suspected the eagles might have a nest. A bulky structure, five feet wide and four feet deep, positioned in the forks of a large tree, high above the ground, would be prominent, especially when there were no leaves on the trees. If so obvious, then why had I not spotted one? For my own confidence, I needed evidence a nest was present – even if it were only circumstantial. The sight of the eagle carrying the bluegill head provided that reward.

But, where was the nest? The most obvious conclusion was that the nest must be in a conifer. The upper end of Sand Run Lake is dotted with dozens of red spruce and hemlock trees and clumps of balsam fir and white pine trees. I knew I would need to get close to the conifers to discover a nest. But, I was concerned about disturbing the eagles. I knew any eagles would see me before I saw them. I could only hope they had witnessed humans canoeing, hiking, or cross-country skiing, and had become tolerant.

On March 28, as a late-season snow squall dumped nearly five inches of snow, I conducted yet another nest search. Wind gusts reached 30 mph, as I moved slowly through various conifer stands. Around noon, I spotted a dark mass in the top of a hundred-foot white pine. My expectations climbed significantly. A closer examination with my binoculars confirmed my initial impression. It was indeed a large nest, and almost beyond belief, an adult bald eagle was perched in the nest. I watched the nest for 30 minutes, then retreated to my cabin.

The next morning, my outside thermometer read 4°F. I knew bald eagles could maintain egg temperatures from the high 90s down to below-freezing temperatures.

That afternoon I returned to the nest. Selecting a dense stand of young spruce, a little over 100 yards from the nest, I dropped my insulated foam cushion onto the frozen ground and sat down. An adult eagle was in the nest, standing and feeding two downy-gray eaglets. I was as thrilled as I could ever remember being. Canaan Valley finally had a successful bald eagle nest – at least a potentially successful nest. I would not proclaim it a true success until the eagles were fully grown and flying.

I suspect my actions over the previous two years had played a small role in convincing the eagles to nest in Canaan Valley. But without a doubt, I had played a major role in documenting eagles in the Tucker County valley. If the parents were successful in rearing the eaglets, I would have documented the first successful bald eagle nest in Canaan Valley. There was only a single report of an unsuccessful nest along Sand Run in 2016. In addition, there had been only one prior bald eagle nest reported in Tucker County.

NEST WITH EAGLETS – FINALLY

Talona and Timbre had begun constructing their nest the previous September. Timbre had selected an 80-year old white pine, and strategically positioned the first sticks. The main trunk was arrayed with strong, well-spaced side branches, each offering an inviting foundation for a nest.

Timbre retrieved a fallen limb, three inches thick and four feet long, and positioned it against the main trunk, at the "V" created by a major fork. Two side branches jutted from the main trunk at 45° angles, slightly above the main fork, and provided excellent nest supports. The male lifted dozens of fallen limbs and placed them at the selected location. Talona studied her mate's efforts while roosting a few trees away and flew to a nearby black cherry where she broke off the end of a dead branch. Her addition of the limb to those already positioned by Timbre demonstrated her approval of the site.

The two eagles worked steadily throughout September, adding as many as 20 sticks some days. By the end of the month they had a firm foundation. This shared effort strengthened their bond, and by late autumn they were a dedicated couple. In October they added another 100 sticks, in November nearly 40, and in both December and January an additional 40. The nest-building drive culminated in February when they added 50 sticks. The male brought in twice as many sticks as Talona, but both frequently repositioned larger sticks to maintain nest symmetry.

Although nest building was a shared task, they operated

independently with little cooperation. They frequently passed each other when bringing sticks to the nest and occasionally maneuvered sticks at the same time. On occasion, they attempted to maneuver the same long stick into a desired position – rarely with any success. Eagles lack the coordination and communication skills required to work together in such projects.

The nest 15 feet from the top of the white pine, was four feet wide and over three feet deep. The nest was partially visible from the nearby black cherry trees, but from directly beneath it was nearly impossible to detect.

A pair of bald eagles will utilize as many as 500 sticks in constructing their nest, creating a massive structure. If successful, they continue using it in subsequent years, often adding several hundred sticks each year. Over multiple years a nest can reach a width of 8 feet and a depth of 12 feet. With a weight of 2,000 pounds, these nests are both the largest and the heaviest structure constructed by any bird in North America—only a beaver lodge exceeds it in mass and weight.

A nest consists of a base, an outer raised rim, and a middle bowl. While the base and rim are of sticks, the bowl consists of a softer material. The bowl is somewhat larger than the sitting female's body, measuring three feet in diameter and as much as two feet deep.

To form the bowl, a dozen fistfuls of fallen leaves were brought into the nest monthly, September through December. In January and February this increased to 15, with the female bringing twice as many as the male. The nest's furnishing began to change direction in January when the pair added 20 fistfuls of dried grass. This increased to 30 fistfuls in February to finalize the nest. Talona would often sit in the bowl, shifting forward and backward and side to side, testing and pressing to create the desired shape and depth. Of great importance to Talona was maintaining a firm airy depth of three to four inches, where the eggs would be deposited and remain secure until hatching.

Nest construction fostered the mating urge and the two eagles first copulated on December 24. As the sun rose Talona sidled close to Timbre and brushed his shoulder. When she emitted a quiet chirp, he eagerly hopped onto her back and gripped her wings with his talons. As Talona twisted her tail aside, Timbre brought his cloaca into contact with hers, and ejected a small stream of semen fluid. Numerous sperm immediately began their winding trip through her cloacal chamber, in a race to be the first to reach an egg. Many sperm entered the cloaca of the female but never fertilized an egg. Such is the case with most birds.

This "cloacal kiss," as it is labeled by ornithologists, is the first step in avian insemination. Although somewhat clumsy, and with less than 100 percent efficacy, it seldom fails to produce fertilized eggs. To compensate for this seeming inefficiency, most birds engage in more than one copulation per season. On January 2, Timbre and Talona copulated five times, and by the end of the month had repeated the act 20 times. Temperatures dropped to minus 31°F on January 22, establishing a new historic low for Canaan Valley. The previous recorded low was minus 27°F.

In February, Timbre hopped atop Talona 15 times, often with her encouragement, but always with her approval. Copulation for that nesting season ended with the fertilization of two eggs the second week of February, followed by Talona laying the first egg on February 14 – Valentine's Day – and the next on the 16th.

Talona had become aware of an egg moving down her oviduct 48 hours prior to it actually being laid. Nearly 20 hours were required for the egg shell to form, and this told Talona the big event was nearing. She spent the afternoon of February 13 in the nest, standing at various locations around the rim, staring at the nest bowl, and taking occasional pieces of a bluegill Timbre brought her.

In late afternoon Talona started to rock back and forth, squatted low, and raised the feathers on her head and back of neck. As darkness settled, she widened her stance in the bowl, and intensified her contractions and feather rousing. Shortly after midnight, she forced the egg from her body.

She stood and stared down at the nearly white egg for a few minutes before starting the month-long incubation period. Thin but strong, the calcium carbonate shell, measured three inches in length.

It was important to keep the egg's temperature near 105°F, and to roll it one or two times every hour until hatching. Such movements prevented the delicate blood vessels from adhering to the shell's inner surface. Instinctively, Talona carefully stood astride the egg and pulled it gingerly back under her body with her beak, rolling it in the process. She settled softly onto the egg and with slight side-to-side and front-to-rear motions, she positioned her brood patch directly over the egg. Talona remained on the egg all night but rose every hour to turn it. Each time, she also repositioned her body so she faced a different direction in the nest.

Shortly after daylight, Timbre flew into the nest from the nearby perch where he had spent the night. Talona rose from the egg and invited her mate to replace her. He cautiously dropped down into the bowl, curled his talons beneath his toes, and stepped around the egg. With one foot on each side, he initiated his first official egg roll. Nearly identical to Talona's behavior, he reached out with his beak, hooked it over the egg, and very slowly pulled it back beneath his breast. Within 50 seconds, his own brood patch was firmly atop the egg, duplicating the warmth provided by his mate.

The brood patch is a bare, featherless area on an adult eagle's chest region. Abundantly supplied with blood vessels, the patch transfers heat from the adult to the egg. Without the adult's brood patch, egg temperatures could not be maintained at 105°F.

The pair's second egg appeared at mid-morning the next day. Talona and Timbre quickly fell into the instinctive routine they would follow for 35 days until both eggs hatched. Incubation of the two eggs was shared by both parents, although not equally. Talona remained in the nest throughout the night and rolled her eggs every one-two hours.

Timbre's hunger drove him to initiate frequent large aerial circles above the lake. He spotted several small bluegill and began his dive.

Stooping towards the surface, at a height of nearly 15 feet, he struck the water but missed. Several powerful wing flaps pulled him skyward and he continued his high-elevation search.

He missed three more diving attempts that morning, but in early afternoon, he sunk his talons into the back of a nine-inch bluebill which he took back to the nest. Talona quickly stepped away from the eggs and began tearing off chunks of flesh from the quivering bluegill. Timbre took her place atop their eggs, turned them three times, then settled down. After consuming the bluegill, Talona began her own high-elevation circles. She was seeking exercise and made no effort to find prey. In 20 minutes she returned, replaced Timbre, and resumed her incubation duties for the rest of that afternoon and all the following night.

Pleased to be relieved of her duties the next morning, and anxious to spread her wings, Talona flew to a nearby limb to stretch and observe the surroundings. From there she made a short flight out over the bog before returning to the nest. Landing on the rim of the nest, she stepped into the bowl, and pushed tenderly against her mate's side. Timbre stepped out of the bowl and flew to his nearby perch. Although he would replace Talona four times that day, it was essential he capture her a fish. She had been in the nest all night and had not eaten in over 24 hours.

Neither Talona nor Timbre were able to capture prey on February 18 or 19. On February 20, Timbre knew any prey would suffice, although fish were the most available. Deer and turkey were too large, and songbirds were too small. After sitting silent for two hours, he was tempted to attack a mallard, but the waterfowl never ventured far from clumps of cattails, and the eagle never had a clear path where he could dive undetected at them.

A wide crack had developed in the ice covering much of the lake. A muskrat was using the edge of the ice as a feeding platform, and repeatedly nibbled on a cattail stalk, dived into the water, and then climbed back onto the ice. Muskrats were common in Sand Run Lake, but were rarely vulnerable to attack by an eagle.

They typically swam underwater from their bank den, dug up a cattail root or gathered a short section of stem, and swam to a floating feeding platform. Their raised feeding platforms were usually located in dense shore vegetation, and not readily seen by eagles. Also, muskrats typically feed during evening and nighttime. Hunger and the ice cover, however, forced a few muskrats to feed in the early morning.

The fourth time the muskrat scampered onto the ice, Timbre launched. The muskrat was facing away from the ice crack while nibbling a cattail, and Timbre made a swift glide towards the rodent's rear. Wings set, his shadow raced across the snowy lake until within eight feet when he extended his feet forward. The blow struck the muskrat solidly, driving it onto the slippery ice. Muskrat and eagle slid several yards, before Timbre's outstretched wings halted the skid. Briefly the muskrat struggled, but talons had penetrated its heart.

Lean from winter, the muskrat weighed only two pounds, and Timbre easily took flight with it. He landed on the rim of the nest and Talona stepped away from the eggs and began tearing through the thick brown fur of the belly. After eating the heart and liver, Talona began ripping out large chunks of dark red flesh. The still-warm meat was desperately needed if she were to maintain her own body temperature and that of her eggs. After consuming nearly a pound, she replaced Timbre on the eggs. He ate most of the remaining muskrat flesh, and left the bones and hide near the outer edge of the nest.

An unusual warm front pushed into Canaan on February 23, and temperatures reached 70°F. Ice and snow began to melt and hunting became significantly easier for the eagles. Talona began screeching and gesturing with her head. Emitting over 70 screeches in three minutes, she anxiously welcomed Timbre who flew in clutching a flopping, 13-inch sucker. Talona inserted her lower beak under the gill cover, pulled the fish from her mate and began eating. Gills, jaw bones, brains, and eyes were eaten. Bones, fins, flesh, heart, liver, and stomach were swallowed quickly. The last of the fish was swallowed in large pieces: caudal and pelvic fins, plus backbone and large pieces of flesh. The male sat on a nearby limb while the female enjoyed her feast.

Several inches of snow fell the last week of February, and Talona spent an entire night shaking herself clear of the layers that accumulated on her back. Small amounts of light snow drifted onto the eggs when she stood to rotate them, but she had no difficulty insulating them against the cold. The two eagles had gone three days with nothing to eat when the snow finally stopped falling.

A clear night with no wind brought many nocturnal critters from their dens. Their searches for food were secondary to another goal – locating a potential mate. It was breeding season for foxes, opossums, raccoons, and skunks. But their innate drive to mate made them vulnerable to predators.

Most important to eagles were the opossums. These marsupials ventured forth from their dens both day and night. Timbre was sitting in one of his favorite perch trees, when movement near a fallen beech tree caught his attention. He focused on the patch of grayish-white fur, patiently waiting for it to emerge. Nearly 20 minutes passed before Timbre caught a clear look at the cat-sized critter. It was an opossum, known regionally simply as a possum. With a length of 26 inches, including a tail of 11 inches, it was an attractive target. The possum wandered aimlessly around the fallen beech, constantly sniffing the snow for the scent of a female.

The hungry possum was in a blueberry patch, 15 feet from the fallen tree, when Timbre launched his attack. The eagle had the sun to his back, and the possum never saw him until within 20 feet. Possums cannot move quickly, have no defensive weapons, and are easy prey for most predators. It opened its mouth wide, hissed loudly, but could do nothing else. Talons penetrated the opossum's back, and within seconds it had collapsed. His usual strategy of feigning death to escape was of no value; it was real enough.

The opossum weighed six pounds and was heavier than Timbre

wanted to lift. Thus, he began tearing through the tender belly skin, and into the body cavity. Heart and liver were eaten first, followed by tender white flesh from around the shoulders. After the intestines had been discarded, Timbre gripped the carcass firmly with both feet and arrived at the nest, offering the partially-warm possum to Talona. In 30 minutes little remained except bones and fur.

Embryonic development had begun immediately after Timbre's sperm fertilized the two eggs. Oxygen and carbon dioxide moved freely through the pores of the eggshells, assuring successful cell division and growth. Ten days after laying, the embryonic eaglets had grown to a recognizable shape within their shells. At twenty days, the yolk sacs which provided all the eaglet's nourishment during development, had been absorbed. And so, at 31 days, a small, hard, sharp, calcium tip formed on the tip of the upper beak of each eggshell-imprisoned eaglet. This was the all-important "egg tooth."

Pipping, the act of piercing of the eggshell, must be accomplished by all eaglets, with no assistance from either parent. The membrane enveloping the embryo was first pierced approximately four days prior to hatching. At that time, the chick took its first breath from the air bubble at the end of the shell. Prior to that time, oxygen was transferred to the chick through pores in the eggshell. Energized by the air bubble oxygen, the eaglet was invigorated and began scratching a hole in the shell with its egg tooth.

At 35 days, the eaglet turned slowly inside the shell in a circular path near the rounded end. As the end cap separated from the remaining mass of the shell, the egg tooth almost immediately began drying. Following separation of the end cap, the eaglet began the crucial struggles that eventually led to hatching. It attempted to lift its head, but, exhausted and fighting gravity, it had difficulty doing so. In about three hours, however, it toppled out of the shell.

Wet from fluids within the egg shell, the eaglet's natal down was matted and dark gray. Its skin was pinkish. Its eyes were black. Its toes were pale yellow. The cere, a fleshy bare patch of skin at the base of the beak, was pale gray. The eaglet, weighing a little over ten ounces, had a total length of about six inches. Feeble and wobbling, it rested in the soft grass of the nest and emitted faint peeps.

Three hours after exiting the shell, Canaan Valley's first bald eagle chick raised its bobblehead, opened its eyes, and received its first offer of food by Talona. At about the same time, its egg tooth dropped off. Awkwardly grabbing for the tiny piece of fish flesh, the eaglet missed its first four attempts. The first morsel of semi-solid food was quickly swallowed. During the next few hours, as the eaglet's eyesight sharpened, mother and eaglet became more efficient at transferring morsels of fish. Using its wings as braces, the eaglet slowly gained control of its head and beak, while the mother learned to turn her beak sideways so their beaks met at a 90⁰ angle.

On March 23, the second embryo began rotating in its shell. Shortly after midnight Talona stood, peered closely at the chick and the pipped egg, and emitted several chirps. Moments later, the eaglet tumbled from the shell into the grassy nest bowl. Talona continued studying her two nestlings and gave multiple calls to Timbre who joined his new family. Nearly 15 minutes later, Talona curled her talons beneath her toes, and stepped carefully on opposite sides of her young. With cautious shifting of her weight, she maneuvered the brood patch directly onto the eaglets, dropped her wings onto the dried grass to provide extra insulation, and slowly settled over her offspring in the falling darkness.

A heavy dose of good luck would be required to assure that the nestlings reached the fledgling stage in three months. Newly-hatched eaglets are nearly helpless. Such young are labeled "altricial" in contrast to those capable of finding and capturing their own food, which are "precocial." Newborn eaglets are not capable of maintaining a constant body temperature and their eyes are not functional at hatching. Though warm-blooded, it takes about 10 to 14 days for their down feathers and blood circulation to develop to maintain their own body heat. It is essential that their parents continue to transmit their own body heat to their eaglets after hatching.

The journey from hatchling to fledgling would be fraught with foodless days, blowing snow, freezing rain, and attacks by owls, hawks, and bears. But, there also would be pleasant days when parents and eaglets had stomachs filled with fish, the sun was warm, and breezes blew out of the south. There would be days when white billowy clouds drifted across a pale blue sky when new-born fawns played in meadows of goldenrod and when newly-hatched turkey poults chased grasshoppers through blueberry patches.

RAISING A FAMILY

Two mornings after the hatching of eaglet number two, raucous calling of the local crow family alerted both parents to potential food. Talona remained on the eaglets while Timbre investigated. He watched as five crows made numerous food-caching trips from an animal carcass. A coyote had killed a winter-weakened deer the previous night. After eating, he had returned to his den where he fed his mate and her pups a meal of regurgitated venison.

One of the crows had discovered the deer shortly after daybreak. In less than 30 minutes, his flock (mate and three previous year's young) had eaten and began caching deer flesh. Flying 20 to 50 yards from the carcass, each crow independently selected a patch of grass or small blueberry bush where it poked the meat out of sight. Known for their fabled memories, crows can remember the locations of most such cache sites for several months. On some future day when no food was available, they would revisit the sites and get an easy meal.

Timbre alighted about ten feet from the carcass, took several cautious awkward steps, and hopped atop the carcass. His beak helped him to pull off larger and tougher chunks than could the crows. The beak of a crow is straight and pointed, while that of an eagle is strongly hooked. As a result, an eagle can separate chunks of muscular meat from a carcass much easier than can a crow. After hopping off the dead whitetail, he took a drink then flew directly back to the nest. Unlike coyotes, and many other birds of prey, eagles are unable to regurgitate food.

Although bald eagles have no form of vocal communication, Talona was aware that Timbre had eaten. She noticed his distended crop, and detected deer meat on his breath. She had watched his direction of travel, and she was soon soaring towards the carcass. Timbre assumed an insulating position atop the two eaglets and settled down to digest his meal.

Instinct told the two parents that they must obtain food for their young, but instinct also told them to first satisfy their own hunger. The death of a parent due to starvation would also result in the demise of the young.

Three days later, with much of the venison having been eaten, Timbre pushed off toward the Blackwater River. A few largemouth bass were cruising below the dam, and were closely studied by Timbre. Although three dives by the male eagle proved fruitless, the fourth produced a 12-inch fish.

Talona spotted her mate approaching the nest and stepped away from the eaglets even before Timbre landed in the nest, and almost before he released his hold she was tearing at the fish. Only when her hunger had been satiated did she feed the eaglets. Still not strong enough to move their bodies, all they could do was raise their wobbly heads and open their beaks.

Although only two days older than her brother, the female eaglet, hereafter to be known as Dahlee, was clearly stronger and more coordinated. As a result, she raised her head higher and her beak wider. Talona responded to the eager mouth and offered the first 12 chunks of fish to Dahlee. Only when her crop was nearly full did Talona offer any to the male eaglet. Because the eaglets and their crops were still relatively small and their heads were relatively large, they soon were satiated and ceased begging for food. With more than half the fish remaining, Talona had a few more bites.

Later that day as a snow squall blew, Talona stepped away from the eaglets to the bass carcass. All remaining flesh was removed and fed to the eaglets, with Dahlee receiving nearly twice as much as brother, Leuca. When only the backbone, pectoral fins, and caudal fin remained, Talona swallowed each whole.

Nighttime temperature dropped into the teens on March 29. During the first week of the eaglets' lives Talona and Timbre were challenged to capture enough fish to feed their nestlings. One day neither parent was able to capture a fish, and the eaglets experienced their first extended hunger which resulted in increased aggressive behavior. Dahlee frequently struck at her little brother with her beak. Her painful blows were aimed at his head and caused Leuca to assume a defensive stance, with head held between his legs. Only when facing away from his big sister, in a defensive posture, did the blows from Dahlee cease.

As the second consecutive day passed without food, Timbre drifted eastward. Red Creek and other small streams draining the Sods were frozen so Timbre focused on rabbits and hares. Snowshoe hares were absent in Canaan Valley, and cottontail rabbits were rare, living mainly in yards and gardens which were avoided by eagles. Dolly Sods, however, supported small populations of New England cottontails and snowshoe hares. Cottontails spent the day in ground burrows or beneath shrubs. Snowshoe hares sought refuge under the low, sprawling branches of red spruce trees, but ventured out when their own hunger pangs increased.

Although the furry coats of snowshoe hares had transformed from summer brown to winter white, their three-pound bodies threw visible shadows on the snowy landscape when they moved. Within 30 minutes, Timbre initiated a sharp dive. A juvenile hare had not yet learned that danger is ever-present. Timbre's impact crumpled the hare. Large clumps of fur were torn off as were the intestines.

Timbre sunk the talons of one foot into the back of the hare, and began the short trip home. The still-warm flesh was joyously received by Talona, and she ate before feeding the eaglets. Dahlee dominated her brother, and 35 minutes passed before Leuca was allowed to eat. Fortunately, this time the hare was large enough to provide adequate food for him.

Not only did the adult eagles frequently bring food to the nest, but they actively refurbished it with grasses, leaves, and moss, plus additional support sticks. Clumps of dried leaves and grass had been deposited into the center of the nest almost daily from January to March, providing cushioning and insulation. Subsequently, a daily activity of Talona involved aerating the nest bowl. She would insert her beak deep into the bottom of the bowl, grasp a clump of compressed nesting material, pull it up, and scatter it around the bowl.

By two weeks of age, the eaglet's gray down feathers were growing fluffier, and necks and wings were growing stronger. Extended wings and the overly-large rump area formed a sturdy tripod, enabling the eaglets to hold their still-wobbly heads nearly straight up. Skin around the eyes had turned light gray, as had that of the cere. The rictus, the corner of the mouth where the fleshy area of the upper and lower beaks meet, had become pale yellow. The most prominent change involved the downy covering. Small, black pin feathers had started to emerge. Dahlee by now weighed nearly two pounds, but her brother weighed noticeably less.

April brought a short bout of spring weather to Canaan and the eagles' fishing success improved. Air temperatures reached the 80s on several days and Talona and Timbre captured fish almost daily. The two eaglets added size and strength. For their part, the parents made no effort to see that they received equal food. The nestling that raised its head highest and opened its beak widest typically received the most pieces of fish. And that was always Dahlee.

When a fish was brought to the nest and Talona was tearing off small pieces, Dahlee continued her aggressiveness towards her brother. To escape her strikes to his head, Leuca moved behind his mother and peered out from between her legs. In that position he was somewhat protected and could receive an occasional bite from Talona. While Dahlee usually could consume enough to fill her crop, Leuca often was not able to do so. A smaller fish brought to the nest would be completely eaten and the male eaglet would still be hungry.

The second week of April, Timbre discovered the den of a groundhog. He spotted the brown mammal kicking clumps of earth from beneath the roots of a nearby red maple. The young male had been born the previous summer, from a late litter, and was only half grown. After emerging from nearly five months of hibernation, the skinny rodent searched for green vegetation to eat. Unfortunately, at that time of year, Canaan Valley had little to offer. During periods of inclement weather, the groundhog, or woodchuck as it is also called, remained asleep in its deep earthen den.

Timbre watched the den opening for several days, until one afternoon the groundhog ventured a stone's throw from the den opening. With its back to Timbre, it focused on a tempting clump of greening ferns. Timbre launched his attack with only two wing strokes and quickly penetrated its lungs and heart. Timbre rolled the rodent onto its back so he could rip open the tender skin beneath the shoulder and was soon eating. Next he pulled out and discarded the unwanted intestines. After he had consumed about a pound of flesh, he took the hairy rodent to his family.

As usual, Talona saw Timbre approaching and emitted several high-pitched screeches. Talona rose from her nestlings and the entire family watched eagerly as Timbre landed and dropped dinner. The groundhog was large enough that Talona, Dahlee, and Leuca all had their fill.

After Dahlee filled her crop, and while her mother was feeding her brother, she changed her position in the nest so her rump was facing the rim. She dropped her head to the grassy bowl, elevated her rump as high as possible, and squirted a white stream of fecal material out over the rim of the nest.

Food swallowed by eagles passes through the mouth into the crop, where it is stored until digestion can begin. A short time after eating, food moves from the crop into the stomach where chemical breakdown begins. Items that cannot be digested, such as bones, feathers, and scales, are regurgitated out of the mouth as oval-shaped pellets. The firmly-packed pellets regurgitated by adults are approximately two by three inches in size, while those of eaglets are rarely longer than one-half inch.

The final process in digestion is expulsion of the remaining semi-liquid out of the anal opening. Despite their precarious perches, it is highly unusual for adult eagles or their nestlings to dirty their nest. Adults expel their white streams as much as ten feet away from the nest, while nestlings can expel their white streams up to three feet beyond the nest.

This is one of many instinctive behaviors that is inexplicably passed from generation to generation, with no formal teaching or training. Building a nest is also instinctive, but one could argue that every adult was imprinted with what a nest looks like. Likewise, one could argue that eaglets can watch their parents eject streams, and "learned" accordingly. However, there is little reason to believe this actually happens. We are left with only instinct as an explanation for this amazing behavior.

At around three weeks of age, when nestlings have attained a high degree of thermoregulation, adults can leave them exposed to the elements for short periods of time. However, late season snowstorms, or strong winds and cold rains trigger the protective instincts of adults.

Despite their elevated nest, the world of young eaglets is extremely limited. They remain in the bowl all day, moving only a few inches when food is brought. Their early lives primarily involve sleeping and eating and they have little awareness of the world beyond their nest. The rim of the nest blocks their view, and overhead leaves and limbs obstruct the sky. They learn to identify their parents within 24 hours, although they are slow to distinguish their mother from their father. Their eyesight slowly develops over the first two weeks, but no objects other than that of their parents are recognized.

By the end of April, when nearly four weeks old, the eaglet's talons turned black, the rictus is yellow, the feet are pale yellow, and the flight feathers of the wing are finally prominent. Eyesight, too, is greatly improved. Weight of Dahlee was over six pounds, but that of Leuca only five pounds. Each had acquired the muscle strength and coordination to stand and began shuffling around the bowl.

Also continuing would be the competitiveness between Dahlee and Leuca. Female eaglets are typically larger, and if a female hatches first, her dominance will grow. It is not unusual for a smaller and weaker male eaglet to be shoved out of a nest by a larger sister.

LATE STAGES OF DEVELOPMENT

In April leaves were unfolding and bright green stems of bracken and interrupted ferns were visible. American toads were trilling and spring peepers were peeping. A pair of American kestrels, also known as sparrow hawks, were performing courtship flights near the nest box erected by a homeowner. Pairs of Canada geese had returned from their wintering along the North Carolina coast and were defending their nest sites. Eggs would soon follow. The only remaining snow occurred in small patches on the ski slopes of Timberline. There would be a few more nights when temperatures dipped below freezing, but plants and animals were convinced winter had ended.

By the end of April, at nearly five weeks of age, the two eaglets were regularly stretching and flapping wings and preening growing feathers. By now, their yellow feet seemed outsized, having grown to nearly full size and they confidently moved around the bowl and rim of the nest. Often left unattended for 40 minutes or more, the siblings now maintained a constant body temperature of near 104°F. Their world had slowly expanded as they grew aware of a variety of birds that shared the space around their nest.

The eaglet's occasionally stepped onto the rim and got a view of the forest. Blue jays, chickadees, and titmice almost daily flew close to the nest or landed on a nearby limb. With each such encounter, the eaglet's world slowly began to expand.

One morning the eaglets detected a male ruffed grouse, strutting atop a fallen quaking aspen log. With neck feathers ruffled and wings out swept, the drumming grouse was attempting to attract a female. The eaglets watched in fascination as the performance continued for nearly an hour. Their attention was then drawn to a pileated woodpecker. Then the eaglets settled in and began their morning nap.

Each spring most wildlife were in a critical stage of their annual reproductive cycle. A few, such as coyotes and foxes, had already produced young-of-the-year, while others would delay birth or hatching until conditions were more suitable. May was the final month for the young of most mid and large-sized vertebrates to enter the world.

For bald eagles, hatching in March meant fledging in June, when prey was abundant. Two groups of fish began annual reproduction earlier than did most other aquatic species in Canaan Valley. In April, when water temperatures reached 65°F, suckers and catfish initiated their annual spawning rituals. Redhorse suckers were the first to move from Sand Run Lake into its feeder tributaries. These fish were searching for shallow gravel areas where eggs could be deposited and fingerlings would have adequate food and cover. Adult suckers were vulnerable to predation at this time, and provided a reliable food source for bald eagles.

In May, brown bullhead catfish began moving from the lake into tributaries searching for spawning habitat. Ideally, they wanted a sandy stream bottom beneath an overhanging log. Sand substrate was optimum for depositing eggs, with oxygen levels high enough to assure survival of embryos.

One Sand Run female bullhead selected a site beneath a fallen red spruce. She cleared silt and mud from the sand and gravel in a shallow depression for her eggs. She was soon joined by a male. The four-year old female was 12 inches long and weighed two pounds, while the male was about 15 inches long and weighed three pounds. These spawning bullheads were an ideal size for eagles.

The catfish formed a monogamous pair, sharing duties of the underwater nest, protecting eggs and newly-hatched fingerlings. The pair assumed a side-by-side position, suspended near the bottom, but facing in opposite directions. As the female released eggs, the male released sperm. A tight small ball, about the size of a baseball and with nearly 200 fertilized eggs settled onto the sandy stream bottom.

Timbre detected three male bullheads circling above their nests. Each was within 12 inches of the water surface, and extremely vulnerable to a foraging eagle. One ventured away from the suspended nest log, and when it temporarily halted swimming, Timbre launched and plunged his talons into the water with a great splash. Two talons penetrated the bullhead's neck, while two hit just behind the sharp, venomous spine located within the dorsal fin. Fish and bird were momentarily thrust deep into the pool. Moments later, Timbre was flapping to his nest, transporting a flopping catfish.

Talona spotted Timbre over 300 yards away and started a raucous screeching. After satisfying her own hunger, Talona began feeding the nestlings. The fish was large enough to satisfy all three eagles, but left nothing for Timbre. As evidenced by nearly two dozen catfish skulls beneath the nest, Timbre would make numerous other bullhead captures that spring.

Several pairs of Canada geese had laid their eggs by the end of April. Ganders now cruised the lake, constantly defending against other geese and any potential nest predators. By the middle of May, goslings began to appear. Parents remained with their goslings 24 hours per day. Parents did not directly feed their goslings, but led them to the choicest, most tender young green growth. Newly-hatched goslings are capable of walking and running, and eating with no help from their parents.

Adult geese and their goslings kept busy throughout daylight hours, nipping off tips of green growth. At night they ventured out into the lake, where they remained until the next morning. Geese are good swimmers, with dense down feathers keeping them afloat with little effort. The middle of a lake was a much safer site than any place on shore.

Both Talona and Timbre spent hours studying the geese. When first hatched, the greenish-yellow goslings were too small to interest the eagles. However, once grown to the size of a pigeon, they became a potential meal. One cloudy day in May, a pair of geese with their four goslings was feeding in short grass atop the earthen dam. When one of the more independent goslings ventured nearly eight feet away from her parents, Talona vaulted into the air. Her dive quickly brought her within 20 feet of the geese before the adults detected her attack. They both gave out an alarm squawk and scurried towards the water. The adults plopped into the water with three gosling close behind. The fourth gosling heard her parents' alarm but could not see their wild run for the water. Talona struck as the gosling frantically topped the breast of the dam. In the natural world some young are sacrificed so others can survive, and so it was that day.

Talona presented her eaglets with their first gosling meal. Dahlee had already begun grabbing prey brought to the nest. Although the gosling skin was relatively thin, Dahlee could not rip it open. The greenish-yellow down feathers bothered her and made her hesitant to continue the attack. Sensing her failure, Talona stepped onto the gosling and neatly severed a small wing for Dahlee. Dahlee struck her brother twice in the back of the head, and her sharp beak brought a large drop of blood to his feathers. Leuca finally got a bite when he was offered the intestines. In less than two minutes, nothing remained.

By the second week of May, the eaglets were 75 percent grown. Dahlee weighed over eight pounds, while Leuca weighed just under seven. They were brownish black, with most juvenile feathers fully erupted from their sheaths. Wing flapping was becoming vigorous, and they attained lift-off several times each day. They elevated four to six inches, but made no attempt at flight. Parents left them alone for long periods of time and the nestlings had begun standing on the perimeter of the nest, observing life in the surrounding forest.

By the end of April, Talona quit attending her eaglets. Only when the weather was severe did she spend the night huddled over them. Other nights, both Talona and Timbre slept in a nearby spruce.

The night of May 13 the two eaglets were huddled alone. Around midnight, both adults were awakened by the scratching of claws on the bark of the nest tree. Instantly on full alert, Timbre flew to the nest tree. Talona began screeching. Timbre could hear the invader moving but could not identify it. He flew to the rim of the nest and peered over the edge. He could see nothing, although the sounds were coming nearer — the danger ascending upward in the darkness.

A family of flying squirrels had occupied the base of the nest since March, and a litter of the small soaring squirrels that could glide, though not fly, disturbed the sleep of eagles many nights. Timbre knew this was something considerably larger. The invader attempted to push its way through the barrier of sticks forming the base of the nest, but the wall of tightly woven sticks halted progress. Timbre sensed the predator circling around the tree trunk, and adjusted his own position so he was directly above.

The threat was a raccoon who was searching for food for her kits. The scent of white fecal splashing that encircled the trunk of the nest tree caught her attention. As she climbed the tree, she picked up the odor of fish. The raccoon had not detected the eaglet scent until half way up the tree. Weighing nearly 15 pounds, the raccoon was capable of killing the eaglets. However, she would hesitate to attack Timbre, even though she outweighed him by five pounds.

The instant the mother raccoon eased over the rim of the nest, Timbre attacked. The six-foot span of his flaring wings and his high-pitched screams frightened the raccoon and it beat a hasty retreat, narrowly escaping the strike of a lethal beak. Talona arrived at the nest and took a defensive position near the eaglets. The raccoon scampered face-first down the tree trunk. That threat was neutralized, but the young eagles would face more before they were flying free.

Memorial Day brought vacationers to Sand Run Lake, and as many as six canoes and kayaks cruised the lake at one time. While standing on the rim of their nest, Dahlee and Leuca could see large portions of the lake. Fortunately, they were over 600 yards from the bright colored kayaks, which caused them no fear. The eaglets studied the kayaks with considerable curiosity, just as the hikers, who passed within 200 yards of the nest, studied the eaglets.

Most entertaining to the young eagles were the daytime activities of numerous nesting birds. They studied a family of crows and learned they had nothing to fear from them. Ravens and turkey vultures often soared high over their nest. A pair of kestrels were raising a family in a nest box. Although nearly 500 yards away, the excellent eyesight of the eaglets enabled them to watch the frequent visits of the falcon parents, as they daily brought eight to ten small rodents or shrews to their hungry nestlings.

"Wood pecking" was common in trees around their nest, as downy, hairy, red-bellied, and pileated woodpeckers added to the cacophony of sounds. Most unique was the repetitive pecking of yellow-bellied sapsuckers. More persistent than most woodpeckers, sapsuckers constantly operated on trunks of beech, maples, and conifers in an attempt to keep sap flowing from the small holes they had created.

Venturing through nearby fields, constantly on the alert for grasshoppers or other insects, broods of turkey poults and grouse chicks accompanied their mothers. Ducklings and goslings likewise accompanied their mothers, but always in or near water. But no matter how fascinating and tempting, all the eaglets could do was watch.

One day, a homeowner placed a road-killed opossum along the shoreline. The owner had been hearing a coyote chorus and wanted to photograph them, but the local family of crows spotted the carcass the next morning. Two hours after sunrise, a lone turkey vulture investigated the crow activity. It circled lazily, high above the crows for nearly 15 minutes before being joined by a second, and then a third, vulture. By nine o'clock, seven vultures were circling. Fifteen minutes later the kettle of vultures had brought their circle to the ground, surrounding the opossum carcass. While a vulture is nearly three times the size of a common crow, a crow family will continue eating when a single vulture flies in. However the mass of vultures was overwhelming and the crows retreated as the bigger birds landed.

The tables were turned when Timbre arrived about 40 minutes later. The keen-eyed vultures immediately abandoned their feast. Timbre circled once and landed a yard from the roadkill. Unfortunately, little remained. The opossum had been ripped open along its right shoulder when hit by the pickup truck, and so even the crows had no difficulty making inroads into the carcass. What they started, the vultures finished. All that remained for Timbre was mostly a dirty gray hide and a tangle of shiny white bones.

Every autumn, most turkey vultures left Canaan Valley. Thus, competition at animal carcasses was nearly eliminated by November. Only coyotes, crows, and an occasional red-tailed hawk competed with eagles during winter. By May, turkey vultures were again a major competitor. Carcasses of deer, hefty grass carp, raccoons, or any other large or mid-sized animal would rarely persist longer than 48 hours. Fortunately for bald eagles, young-of-the year of other prey animals were available and relatively easy to capture.

By the first week of June, the eaglets were nearly full-grown. Each had reached its adult weight and their flight feathers, in fact, were longer than those of their parents. Dahlee also weighed several ounces more than her mother, while Leuca weighed less than his father. Only their beaks and talons were not fully grown. Both birds frequently hopped along one particular limb close to their nest, with an occasional flight of four to five feet. Their landings were awkward, but neither eaglet fell to the ground. Two limbs that served as part of the nest's foundation rose at 45° angles and provided strong, yet awkward perching for the eaglets.

The nest of a pair of bald eagles is often referred to as an eyrie. However, an eyrie consists of more than a nest. It includes the limbs that support the nest and provide comfortable perches for adults during incubation. Such proximate perches are used during daylight hours by one parent while the other is incubating eggs. After incubation, these horizontal side branches are also used by one parent while the other is huddling over the eaglets.

These same heavy limbs, projecting upward through the sides of the nest, are an integral component of the eaglets training grounds. Walking out onto these limbs, and later jumping from one to another, constitutes early flight exercises.

Unfortunately, a white pine isn't an ideal environment for eaglets engaged in flight training. A mature hardwood is much better. Beech, cherry and maples all have multiple, nearly-horizontal limbs for an eaglet to hop, jump, and practice short flights. Pine trees offer few large horizontal limbs void of side branches in the upper half of the tree, and an eagle's nest is typically located within 15 feet of the top.

One of the key steps in eaglet maturation involves strengthening the gripping power of their toes and talons. This can best be accomplished by perching on four-inch thick horizontal limbs within the eyrie. Gripping a limb prepares them for perching safely during high winds, and also for gripping prey.

By June, Dahlee weighed eleven pounds, while Leuca weighed only eight. Leuca was noticeably less coordinated and his landings were more awkward, and he frequently ended up hanging upside down from a limb when he attempted to land. Twice he fell to a limb beneath the nest. Fortunately, the pine had quite a few limbs along its upper trunk, and Leuca was able to return to the nest with short jumps from limb to limb.

Talona and Timbre were absent from the eyrie for hours at a time as the summer solstice approached. Although they were still bringing food to their youngsters, they frequently allowed them to go hungry for two or three days at a time. Being fully grown, the eaglets needed less food than when they were adding weight every day, and the lack of food would encourage them to depart the nest.

Late one afternoon, Leuca attempted a short flight from the nest.

He landed awkwardly, and tumbled to the ground. Horizontal branches around the base of the spruce were so dense Leuca could not get a firm grip on any of them. After several failed attempts, he collapsed wearily against the base of the tree. As shadows began to lengthen, Leuca hopped awkwardly to the base of the nest tree. With no difficulty, he flew onto a dead branch. However, subsequent attempts at moving up to a higher limb were unsuccessful.

Leuca had never spent a day, let alone a night, away from his eyrie and was now facing the unknown. He was physically capable of surviving the night on or near the ground – if a predator did not find him. However, the limb upon which he now perched was only four feet above the ground.

As the sun dropped the low-pitched droning whirr of a diving nighthawk and the eight eerie hoots of a barred owl resonated. White-footed mice, red-backed voles, and flying squirrels began their nightly foraging ventures. Hungry mid-sized nocturnal mammals were also on the move. A clumsy mother opossum, with 12 embryonic newborns in her pouch, rambled within 15 feet of Leuca, but posed no threat. A short-tailed weasel peered from beneath a fallen log, while attempting to discover the scent of a vulnerable red-backed vole. This 10-inch long, 10-ounce heavy predator could have killed Leuca. However, the size of the eaglet was so threatening that the mustelid gave it only a passing glance.

A bobcat or a black bear was a more serious threat. Sensing his aloneness, Leuca hunkered close to the tree trunk. Though his parents were aware of his absence, they could do nothing to assist him. Both Talona and Timbre spent the night on their usual perch limb, near the nest. Their concern was in protecting their one remaining nestling. They would bring Leuca a fish the next day if he survived the night.

The temperature dropped to 48°F that night but Leuca managed to keep warm by crouching against the tree trunk. Shortly before daylight, a potentially dangerous predator passed within 25 feet, but did not detect him. As the hungry predator moved downwind, it picked up Leuca's scent. Although faint, it was enough to cause the predator to change direction and sniff the air. The predator made no sound, and neither Leuca nor his parents were aware of its presence.

The predator was a coyote, and its well-perfected, silent search brought the canine to within six feet of Leuca. She was a three-year old female who had a small amount of timber wolf blood in her veins. Her father had been born in the Adirondack Mountains, to a coyote mother and a timber wolf father. This "coywolf" offspring had wandered south to Dolly Sods where he had mated with an eastern coyote. The resulting litter had been born in a ground den near the northern end of the Sods.

Following the deaths of her mother and three of her siblings, this particular female coyote had mated with a German shepherd/blue tick bear hound. Unfortunately, her carefree mate had abandoned her before the birth of her "coydog" pups and none of the litter survived. The lone female, known as Applacha, subsequently abandoned her den and wandered for nearly a year, attempting to locate the infrequent, tantalizing, distant coyote howls that rolled across the Valley.

Applacha took a cautious step of her 57 pounds towards Leuca. The coyote had never encountered a bald eagle but it did not matter. Most birds tasted the same, and Applacha would have savored a grouse, a turkey, or even a barred owl.

The short stub of a broken pine branch slightly altered the coyote's attack and her jaws snapped shut less than one foot from Leuca. The eaglet squawked and hopped farther out on the limb. Applacha prepared for another attack, changing her position to avoid any other intervening branches. But her attention was diverted by a terrifying form swooping directly towards her. Timbre had heard Leuca's alarm call. Under the waxing moon, he had spotted the coyote and thrust his beating wings directly in the coyote's face.

Timbre had no intention of sinking his talons into the coyote, but instead wanted to frighten it with his wings. Had he sunk his talons into the coyote, he would have been vulnerable to a response attack. Quickwaving fangs and claws would have inflicted injury upon the eagle. And both Timbre and Leuca would most likely have suffered from such an encounter.

Momentarily confused, and now on the defensive, Applacha moved a few feet behind the tree and prepared for another attack. In unison, Timbre and Leuca set off a chorus of loud shrill squawks, while Timbre renewed his wing flaps. The shadowy, six-foot wingspan created the impression of a much larger creature and the coyote retreated. As dawn arrived Applacha emitted a few deep growls and left. The stand-off had lasted over an hour as the opponents made move and counter-move. Leuca had escaped his first serious dilemma, but not his last.

FROM NESTLING TO FLEDGLING

June is an awe-inspiring month in Canaan Valley. March brought hints that winter was departing, and April provided positive proof of its full retreat. May confirmed that spring had definitely arrived. But in June the glistening whites of snow and ice, the shadowy browns of mud, and the blacks of leafless trees were a memory. The Valley was now a verdant landscape. Green dominated, and every shade could be identified. Green is June and Green is the Valley!

Spruce, hemlock, and fir provide the darkest of greens, while aspens add the faintest. Beech, birch, black cherry, and red maple supply all shades in between. Alder, blueberry, viburnum, willow, and other shrubs contribute even more subtle shades of green. Mosses and ferns, cranberries and goldenrod, and numerous grasses of the fields, beaver ponds, and lakes also announce with their hues that spring has finally arrived.

Not to be outdone, even a few animals add a little something to the emerald show. There are green herons and green frogs and green snakes. Some naturalists would argue the most eye-catching thing in Canaan Valley is a newly-shed green snake.

Also present in June are "green-horns," as newly-fledged bald eagles can be aptly described. This term, used to describe the inexperienced, naive, unseasoned, untried, and raw individual, is quite apropos for a four-month old bald eagle. Five to six years must pass before a green-horn will mature and attain its distinctive mature plumage.

The act of fledging in bald eagles is fraught with danger. Leuca had entered the initial danger phase – learning to fly. Both eaglets had survived the nestling stage, thanks to parents who had protected them, but the parental role was nearing an end.

Following his survival from the coyote attack, Leuca flopped from one branch to another and from tree to tree, struggling to find a connect-the-dots route back home. Three days later he finally flapped back into his nest, joining sister Dahlee. There was no joyous reunion, and life continued as it had, yet something new now distinguished the pair. Leuca had gained experience outside their eyrie. Talona and Timbre continued to bring food to the nest for another week, but not always on consecutive days.

The peaceful nights were forgotten the night of June 12, as a lightning storm arrived unlike anything the eaglets had witnessed. The sky darkened and sharp flashes of heat lightning streaked across the sky, brightly illuminating the branches around Leuca and Dahlee. Peals of thunder accompanied each flash and the two nestling eaglets pulled their head deep beneath a wing. The juvenile eaglets were startled by each flash of lightning, but could do nothing to escape.

One morning in June Talona flew from her perch towards Sand Run Lake. Leuca was perched on the rim of the nest and immediately followed his mother. He sailed nearly 40 yards, before losing altitude. Three clumsy wing beats gained him a few feet in elevation, and he spotted a black cherry tree. While his flapping was productive, his steering was not. He had practiced wing flapping thousands of times in the nest. However, he never had the opportunity to learn how to change direction when flying.

With clumsy altering of body position and awkward wing flaps, Leuca modified his flight path enough to reach the black cherry tree. He crashed into the upper branches, but managed to clench his toes and talons around a branch. With frantic wing beats, he tightened his grip and pulled himself upright. In a mix of joy and trepidation, and relief, he studied his surroundings. He could see the nest tree, but felt no urge to return. Instead, he focused on a beaver pond and a mallard and her five ducklings. Although Leuca was hungry, he had no idea how to capture anything.

Leuca remained in the tree all that day, and two more days. His constant calls for food finally brought Talona, who arrived with a small bass. Dahlee, meanwhile, had been fed twice at the nest while Leuca had been absent.

Finally, on June 15, Dahlee followed her brother and fledged from the pine tree eyrie. Her initial flight was a success. A clean, although slightly awkward landing positioned her on a black cherry tree. It was nearly an ideal perch site, and she remained there for two days. However, hunger eventually saw her return to the eyrie. Her parents brought a gosling to the nest one morning and a young groundhog the next day. Their oldest fledgling was well fed.

Dahlee began making multiple practice flights every day, during which time she returned to the nest every evening. On subsequent days, she abandoned the nest and spent entire days and nights on perches around the lake. She remained in the vicinity for all of June and much of July. Her parents fed her several times each week during June, and she eventually made her own initial capture. Flying the lake's length, Dahlee discovered a dead, floating largemouth bass in a small cove. The bass had been injured by a large snapping turtle, and died from the bite three days later. With an awkward grasp Dahlee produced her first personal prey.

Adult bald eagles are successful in capturing fish in only one-third of their dives. For juveniles the success rate is considerably less. Dahlee, inspired by her success, began making attempts on the live fish she saw. After 15 unsuccessful dives at spawning bluegills, Dahlee managed to latch two talons into the back of an eight-inch bluegill. She flew to a lower branch of a nearby maple, where she struggled to balance and awkwardly dismember the fish into bite-size bits. The rest of that day was spent digesting her bluegill meal.

Several bluegill spawning beds were scattered along Sand Run Lake. When Canaan Valley was originally logged in the early 1900s, a narrow gauge railroad had been constructed from Davis to the upper end of the Valley. One set of tracks traversed the eastern side of the valley, paralleling Glade Run and Sand Run. The foundation of the track was composed of coal cinders, and when Sand Run was dammed in 1983, numerous lengthy sections of these cinder beds were covered by shallow lake water.

Male bluegill concentrated at these railroad beds turned spawning beds and in the cinders created dozens of circular depressions where female bluegill visited each May and June. Each male bluegill defended a spawning depression with dorsal fins often cutting the water surface. Such was the tempting situation awaiting Dahlee and Leuca.

In late June, a small school of grass carp was concentrated in a sun-warmed small cove. Dorsal and caudal fins constantly broke the water surface as the huge carp fed on pondweed shoots. Dahlee could see the backs of the fish, many of which were three feet long and nearly 30 pounds in weight. However, she could not see their full length, and thus did not grasp how large they were. The temptation was too great, however, since she had not eaten in two days. She glided directly towards the schooling carp. As bottom feeders, their attention was focused on the lake bed and they did not see the eagle's approach. In fact, the grass carp had outgrown all potential predators and so had nothing to fear when feeding.

Dahlee solidly struck the back of a carp, and the talons of both feet pierced several inches deep. The fish thrashed wildly, pulling the eagle under the water. Dahlee flapped frantically, but had neither the strength nor the skill to control the fish. Risking drowning, the frantic eagle released her talons, pulled free, and flailed to the surface. With difficulty, she moved through the shallows to the shore and hopped onto a partially-submerged log. After considerable preening and resting, her flight feathers dried enough for her to fly awkwardly to a nearby perch.

She had more success three days later. Dahlee spotted the wake of a serpentine-like animal swimming towards an emergent boulder. She watched anxiously, eager to make a successful capture and end her three-day fast. It was a two-foot long snake. Dahlee extended her toes, dropped onto the reptile, and wrapped one set of talons around its body. The snake struggled violently, but was an easy load for the eagle to carry to her perch. As she landed, the snake struck. Numerous sharp teeth sank into the eagle's leg, just above the knee. Although fluffy leg feathers clogged the snake's mouth, the teeth brought blood.

Fortunately for Dahlee, no snake in Canaan Valley was venomous. This one was a northern water snake, possibly the most abundant snake in the Valley. Every body of water supported a population of these aggressive snakes. They readily strike and bite any potential prey within reach.

Dahlee was frightened when the snake struck, and immediately released her grip. As the snake struck the ground, Dahlee again dived. This time, she quickly sank the talons of both feet into its back and her beak into its neck. The snake squirmed and flopped, but inflicted no more bites. Dahlee flew back to her perch and in minutes nothing remained. The eagle's crop was crammed full with snake, and her memory had also been enlarged.

Leuca, meanwhile, had gone eight days without eating, during which time his parents brought him no food. He missed multiple dives at bluegills, but eventually sank his talons into a bass that was cruising along the shoreline. Leuca was unable to take off from the water with his capture and awkwardly plopped into the shallow water. From there he struggled ashore and consumed the bass while standing in a grassy spot. Though he was slowly improving his flying skills, he had yet to develop his fishing abilities. Regardless, he remained alive.

The last week of June brought almost daily lessons. Leuca dove onto a full-grown muskrat – his increasingly powerful talons easily dealing fatal wounds. As he struggled to take off from the lake, he was dragged back into the water. Three times he attempted to clear the water, but each time he flopped back down. He next tried to swim with the wounded muskrat. Using his wings, he slowly rowed his captive towards shore. When nine feet from land, the muskrat got its feet onto a submerged log and broke free. Drained from the episode, Leuca swam ashore, shook himself off, and hopped several feet onto solid ground. He preened for nearly two hours before becoming dry enough to fly to safety. With almost no assistance from his parents, starvation loomed as a distinct possibility.

Even if Leuca's predatory success was sorely lacking, his flying skills showed improvement every day. Unfortunately, thunderstorms occurred daily, and over three inches of rain were dumped on the mountains. Culverts became clogged and drainage ditches along roads carried tons of silt and sediment down off Cabin Mountain, with much of it entering Sand Run Lake. Waters of the lake became muddy brown and fish became invisible to the bald eagles. Dahlee and Leuca were facing a potentially fatal situation.

Talona and Timbre abandoned Sand Run Lake on the second day of its water's chocolate-like turbidity and headed for the deep pools of the Blackwater River, which remained relatively clear. Dahlee watched them depart, but remained attached to the only body of water she had ever known. Twenty-four hours later, Talona brought a small bass to Dahlee. Leuca had not seen his mother bring the fish to Dahlee and likewise had not seen Talona depart the lake. Dahlee remained at Sand Run Lake but her parents brought her no other meals.

Talona followed her normal seasonal pattern and departed Canaan Valley a week after being forced to abandon fishing in Sand Run Lake. A few hours of flying west brought her to the Tygart River where she had spent prior summers. Visiting the numerous deep pools of this slow-moving river, she had no difficulty capturing adequate fish.

Talona's absence triggered Timbre's own departure, and the first week of July found him cruising comfortably over the Cacapon River. Fish were plentiful, as were cottontail rabbits, and Timbre maintained a full crop.

Dahlee remained at Sand Run Lake expecting a parent to bring her a fish. When neither parent appeared, her hunger and the still-muddy lake waters were reasons to fly south into Canaan Valley State Park. She remained there for nearly a week, but succeeded in capturing only a small sucker. By the first week of July, Dahlee had flown to the deep pools of the

Dry Fork River.

Meanwhile, on the third day of muddy water, with no other bald eagles present, a hungry Leuca had flown north to Glade Run. Isolated from the vacation community's runoff, this wetland had remained silt free, and presented a more promising fishing ground for Leuca.

It took three days, but Leuca finally captured a 12-inch largemouth bass and enjoyed his first meal in nearly a week. The following day, Leuca rode a thermal to the rim of Cabin Mountain, which formed the eastern perimeter of Canaan Valley. From there he soared eastward to Grant County. Another short flight brought him within view of a large body of water even further northeast. It was the largest body of water he had ever seen.

Leuca was less than one mile from the broad water and detected two large birds circling. Curiosity carried him closer and he excitedly recognized them as bald eagles. His hunger convinced him that where there were eagles there must also be food. One was a white-headed, white-tailed adult, while the other was an immature. Dusk was fast approaching and Leuca followed the immature eagle into a red maple tree. Although the two juveniles perched on separate limbs, they were only a short distance apart.

At dawn, on the Potomac River watershed, activities around the expansive lake came alive. Two large fishing boats cruised past the perched eagles and moments later a trio of heavily-laden dump trucks roared along a gravel road. But because the other juvenile did not fly, a nervous Leuca likewise remained perched. As the sun rose higher, a flock of noisy crows caught the attention of the two eagles. Within a few minutes, the local eagle flew towards the crows. Leuca carefully studied the flight of the other juvenile. A short time later, the juvenile disappeared from sight but the crows continued circling along the shoreline. Within minutes, even larger birds circled over the same spot. Leuca recognized them as turkey vultures.

Less than an hour later Leuca soared from the maple tree and glided smoothly across the broad lake. Although innately cautious he was also quite hungry. A half dozen crows, two vultures, and the other juvenile bald eagle were feeding on meaty bones.

This was Mt. Storm Lake, a 1,200-acre reservoir, constructed in 1965. Heated by warm water from a coal-producing power plant, the thermal lake created year-round, ice-free water.

As Leuca joined in, the scavenging birds flapped aside and Leuca enjoyed one of the most satisfying meals he had eaten. In less than an hour, the two immature bald eagles had eaten their fill. Leuca followed the eagle to a massive tulip poplar, and they spent the remainder of the day digesting their meals.

At last experiencing consistent foods, Leuca remained at Mt. Storm Lake the remainder of July and all of August. At least twice per month he was attracted to the hidden cove by crows and was often rewarded with a meal from scattered leg bones. However, in September the supply of bones abruptly came to an end. Fortunately, the shallow waters of Mt. Storm Lake were alive with fish and Leuca captured one every few days.

The first male bald eagle to be fledged from a Canaan Valley nest slowly improved his fishing skills while also gaining invaluable experience in how to survive, as did his sister. Although many challenges lay ahead for the first bald eagles to be born in Canaan Valley, they had successfully maneuvered through the most serious trial: the first summer of life.

EPILOGUE

Canaan Valley officially now had its first successful bald eagle nest. Two eaglets had hatched in March 2022 and the two had fledged that June. The parents had proven that it was possible to raise a family in Canaan in spite of the hazardous winter weather. Only time would tell whether their two eaglets survived and reached adulthood. Much would happen during the next five years before they reached sexual maturity. Fewer than half of all bald eagle fledglings survive their first year.

Considerable research would be required to determine whether Talona and Timbre successfully renested in 2023 and later years. Because tagging juvenile bald eagles with uniquely-colored plastic markers is not permitted, the fate of Dahlee and Leuca will never be known.

However, the future of bald eagles in Canaan Valley appears bright – at least at first glance. Because the life expectancy of a bald eagle is 20 to 30 years, the current nesting pair could potentially renest at least 10 more times (through 2032). While the age of the adults nesting along Sand Run is unknown, I have reason to believe they are both less than 10 years old.

In addition to the nesting pair, at least one other adult and one immature frequented Canaan Valley during the latter part of 2021 and most of 2022. The presence of these four eagles should attract additional adults to Canaan and those newcomers could potentially be supplemented by juveniles from either the Mt. Storm nest or the Sand Run nest.

A nesting pair typically defends a territory of only one or two square miles. With Canaan Valley wetlands covering 12 square miles, and the

94

Blackwater River flowing 20 miles, there should be suitable habitat to accommodate at least five more nesting pairs. Providing further assurance is the protection and solitude of the 16,000-acre (25 square mile) Canaan Valley National Wildlife Refuge.

Although adequate area exists to provide geographic territories for as many as six pairs of eagles, the habitat is marginal at best. The prey base is inadequate to comfortably support additional nesting pairs and their offspring. Ice-covered ponds, lakes, and extensive stretches of the Blackwater River provide few fish during January and February. During deepest winter, fish are catchable only in Glade Run, and stretches of the Blackwater River where rapids prevent ice from forming.

Besides limited fish availability in winter, terrestrial prey are also scarce then. No avian or mammalian species are available in adequate numbers in Canaan during winter to sustain growing eaglets. Only in the two large man-made lakes (Spruce Island and Sand Run), a couple large beaver ponds, and short stretches of the Blackwater River can eagles consistently locate and capture fish in winter.

The Blackwater River, Little Blackwater River, North Branch of the Blackwater, and Glade Run meander over 20 miles through the Valley, yet only 15 miles of the main Blackwater provide suitable nesting habitat for bald eagles. The Little Blackwater, North Branch, and Glade Run lack high-quality nesting and foraging habitat.

Given these limiting factors, it is likely that no more than three successful bald eagle nests will occur in any one year throughout Canaan Valley.

In contrast to Canaan Valley, the future for bald eagles in West Virginia appears quite bright. An assessment shows the Mountain State can support at least 200 more pairs. Statewide, a total of 75 active nests were confirmed in 2021, and 81 during 2022. This number is an underestimate because no effort has been made to locate all eagle nests in the state. Even with a systematic effort, only readily-visible nests and those in areas of heavy human traffic are likely to be detected.

The highest known bald eagle nest density in West Virginia occurs along the South Branch of the Potomac River where 38 active nests were located during 2021. In contrast, only 12 nests were located along the Ohio River in 2021. Potential nesting habitat along the South Branch of the Potomac covers fewer than 100 river miles.

The Ohio River flows 256 miles from Chester to Kenova and the majority of this slow-moving river provides high-quality bald eagle habitat. The Ohio's width, with eight locks and their corresponding lengthy pools, supports a high diversity of forage fish to potentially feed eaglets at hundreds of nests. Also, water quality in the Ohio River is improving, assuring a plentiful supply of forage fish for decades to come. Potential nest trees by the thousands exist within sight of the river. Dedicated fisheries biologists with the WVDNR also guarantee the healthy status of fish populations within the Ohio River.

The diversity of potential prey for bald eagles is greater along the Ohio River than for any other body of water in West Virginia. Potential nesting habitat also occurs along the Cheat, Elk, Greenbrier, Gauley, Guyandotte, Kanawha, Little Kanawha, Monongahela, New, Tug Fork, and Tygart. Undoubtedly, there are several active bald eagle nests along many of these rivers that have not been reported to the WVDNR.

At least six man-made lakes in West Virginia provide suitable habitat for eagle nesting as well. Although there are no natural lakes in West Virginia due primarily to the failure of glaciers to reach this far south, there is no lack of suitable nesting habitat along impounded waterways for bald eagles here.

Population growth of West Virginia bald eagles has been, and will be, restricted by multiple mortality factors. During the decades prior to 1972, DDT was a major limiting factor for bald eagles. This chemical was widely-used in agriculture, and the subsequent runoff provided a pathway for it to reach rivers and bays. Fish became contaminated, and the deadly chemical slowly accumulated in the majority of surviving bald eagles. Egg shell thinning resulted, and only a few eggs successfully hatched. These effects of DDT would ultimately be brought to light by the publication of *Silent Spring*, whose author, Rachel Carson, spent much of her life in watersheds West Virginia shares with Maryland, Ohio, and Pennsylvania. Unfortunately, in the near future, lead poisoning, anti-coagulant rodenticide poisoning, intentional shooting, and accidents will also prevent many juveniles from reaching sexual maturity.

Lead poisoning results from eagles feeding on gut piles of hunter-killed deer, on deer shot by hunters but not recovered, and on varmints such as groundhogs, shot and abandoned by hunters or farmers. Bullets commonly used to hunt deer, bear, and varmints are composed of a lead core and a copper covering. Upon striking an animal, much of the lead disintegrates into small, almost microscopic, particles. Eagles ingest these particles when consuming these animals and subsequently suffer from, and often succumb to, lead in their system. Until lead bullets are made illegal for all forms of hunting, lead poisoning will remain a major mortality factor – although little acknowledged – for our nation's symbol.

Anti-coagulant rodenticides also pose a secondary poisoning threat to bald eagles. These chemical deterrents currently receive wide-spread use by humans to control unwanted small pests – primarily house mice, black rats, and Norway rats. Secondary poisoning results when eagles consume rodents that died from an anti-coagulant rodenticide or when an eagle captures and consumes rodents that had recently consumed non-lethal amounts of a rodenticide.

Shooting of eagles is illegal in the United States. Regardless, several bald eagles are shot each year in West Virginia. A few of the injured are discovered and taken to raptor rehabilitation centers, but the majority die undetected. While some of the targeted eagles might have been misidentified by shooters, others most likely were aware when the shooter pulled the trigger. Whether an eagle is misidentified as a black vulture, turkey vulture, hawk, or owl, it is illegal to shoot any large raptor. All are federally protected by the Migratory Bird Treaty Act of 1918.

Potentially fatal encounters with humans are ever present. An adult female bald eagle was shot in December 2022, near Harman, ten miles south of Canaan Valley. Although the eagle survived the gunshot, it was necessary to amputate its wing tip to save its life. Dr. Jesse Fallon, veterinarian with the Avian Conservation Center of Appalachia, who conducted the surgery, discovered metal fragments in its wing. Due to this criminal act, the eagle will spend its remaining years in captivity. Shooting a bald eagle is a violation of the Bald and Golden Eagle Protection Act, and can result in a fine of up to $100,000 and imprisonment for one year.

Eagles are also killed by striking utility lines, or by being struck by vehicles when flying across highways. Scavenging of road-killed deer makes eagles vulnerable to vehicular accidents. As bald eagle numbers increase, the number struck by vehicles will also increase. To compound matters even further, due to fewer hunters, deer numbers will likely increase into the future. Subsequently, more deer will mean more road kills, which will mean more eagle-vehicle accidents.

A major factor affecting future population growth is the degree of habituation by eagles to humans and their built environment. Fear of humans will gradually lessen, based on the history of habituation by several "wilderness" or near-wilderness species, such as black bear, coyotes, mountain lions, timber wolves, and wild turkey. All of these have apparently lost fear of humans and frequently forage near human dwellings.

There seems little doubt that within the next 20 years bald eagles in West Virginia will forage and build nests much closer to humans. This development has been witnessed in Alaska and will likely result in an increase in mortality for all age classes of eagles in our state. Likewise, greater foraging near industrial complexes, sanitary landfills, and agricultural buildings will expose eagles to secondary poisoning from anti-coagulant rodenticides.

On a positive note, fisheries biologists with the WVDNR have made tremendous progress in increasing fish populations throughout West Virginia, and more improvement can be expected. Thanks to that shift, numbers of bald eagle nests in West Virginia should continue to increase at a steady rate. Likewise, westward dispersal of fledgling eagles from the Chesapeake Bay region will supplement production of eagles from West Virginia nests.

While lead poisoning, anti-coagulant pesticide poisoning, shooting, and accidents will result in the deaths of hundreds of bald eagles, overall population appears to be on a steady upward increase. Canaan Valley has already witnessed improved biological diversification as a result of an influx of bald eagles, and will present a healthier and more stable ecosystem as eagle numbers continue to increase.

With these and other supportive changes, the future looks promising for these majestic raptors. May eagles ever soar through Canaan Valley skies!

POSTSCRIPT

In December 2022, I observed a pair of adult bald eagles engaging in courtship behavior for nearly two hours in a black cherry tree along the western shoreline of Sand Run Lake. Their intimate shoulder rubbing, beak tapping, and neck extensions were convincing indications they were a bonded, permanent pair. In January 2023, I studied them again through my 30X spotting scope, as they fed on the rib cage of a winter-killed deer near Sand Run Lake. In February, the female was sitting in the successful 2022 nest, while the male was perched nearby. Presumably, these birds were Talona and Timbre.

With the discovery and documentation of a productive bald eagle nest in Canaan Valley, I have now checked off a major item on my bucket list. Only one major item remains – the sighting of a mountain lion in West Virginia. For nearly 40 years, I have harbored hopes of spotting a long-tailed big cat in Canaan Valley or on Dolly Sods. Although I once discovered the partially-eaten carcass of a dead deer, with long scratch marks indicative of a cougar, I remain unconvinced that it was evidence of a mountain lion.

Frankly, I want to see a living cougar – preferably before it sees me.

But if that never happens, I will be content with my eagle experiences. They comprise the most satisfying chapter in a very fulfilling career as a wildlife biologist. These observations were as up close and personal as a person could wish for when it comes to experiencing the majesty and life complexities of our nation's symbol of freedom and strength.

BIBLIOGRAPHY

Bailey, Richard S. and Casey B. Rucker. *The Second Atlas of Breeding Birds in West Virginia*. University Park: Pennsylvania State University Press, 2021.

Davis, Jack E. *The Bald Eagle: The Improbable Journey of America's Bird*. New York: Liveright Publishing Corp., 2022.

Gerrard, Jon M., and Gary R. Bortolotti. *The Bald Eagle: Haunts and Habits of a Wilderness Monarch*. Washington, D.C.: Smithsonian Institution Press, 1988.

Gerrard, Jon M., and T. N. Ingram (Eds). *The Bald Eagle in Canada*. Headingley, Manitoba: White Horse Plains Publishers, 1985.

Herrick, Francis H. *The American Eagle: A Study in Natural and Civil History*. New York: D. Appleton-Century Co., 1934.

Laycock, George. *Autumn of the Eagle*. New York: Charles Scribner's Sons, 1973.

Patent, Dorothy H. *Where the Bald Eagles Gather*. New York: Clarion Books, 1984.

Tekiela, Stan. *Bald Eagles: The Ultimate Raptors*. Alabama: AdventureKEEN, 2021.

Wolfe, Art. *Bald Eagles: Their Life and Behavior in North America*. New York: The Crown Publishing Group, 1997.

About The Author

Dr. Michael is a native West Virginian. He was born on Plum Run, in Marion County, near Mannington and Farmington, attended elementary school in Shinnston, and graduated from Magnolia High School in New Martinsville. He received a B.S. degree in Biology from Marietta College, and M.S. and PhD. degrees in Wildlife Ecology from Texas A&M University. He taught at West Virginia University from 1970 through 1997. His 50-year career as a wildlife biologist produced more than 100 publications, both scientific and popular.

Dr. Michael continues to be an active outdoorsman, researcher, and writer, concentrating his efforts on the wildlife of the Appalachian Mountains. Recent products of his writing included: *The Coyotes of Canaan, The Last Appalachian Wolf, Wild and Wonderful: The Wildlife of West Virginia, Death Visits Canaan, Shadow of the Alleghenies,* and *A Valley Called Canaan.*

Made in the USA
Columbia, SC
09 February 2025

53251795R00061